His

Brenda Rothert

His
Copyright © Brenda Rothert 2016
Published by Silver Sky Publishing Inc

Cover designer and Photographer:
Sara Eirew
www.saraeirew.com

Editor:
Lisa Hollett, Silently Correcting Your Grammar

Interior Design and Formatting:
Christine Borgford, Perfectly Publishable
www.perfectlypublishable.com

Prologue

September 28, 2001

Andrew

SEVENTEEN DAYS AGO, my life caught fire.

Two planes. Two towers. Nothing will ever be the same.

The fire at Ground Zero is still burning, and somewhere inside the smoky piles of rubble is my father. Do I want them to find him? For the first week, I did. I stayed home from school every day and stared at the TV, praying I'd see them pull my dad from what's left.

I told myself over and over that he couldn't be gone. David Wentworth was too strong to be taken down like that. He'd show them all. My dad would come crawling out of the pile of debris, still wearing his dark suit. He'd probably pull other people out, too. My dad is like that. He does things people say are impossible.

But the second week, my mom said I had to go back to school. When I told her I wouldn't go because I was waiting for my dad to be rescued, her shoulders fell.

"He's gone, Andrew."

"You don't know that. Dad's a fighter."

She shook her head. "I know it's hard for a thirteen-year-old to wrap his head around. I know. You want him to be here, and I do, too. But he's gone. It's just you and me now."

I glared at her, my throat burning. How could she give up on him like that? I'd never give up on my dad. I went back to my spot in his favorite leather chair in our living room and turned up the news on TV.

But after two weeks, my school counselor came to our house to see me. He frowned and told me no one could survive for two weeks in there. Then he gave me a pamphlet titled, *"It's Okay to Cry."* I crumpled up his advice on grieving and threw it in the trash.

I wasn't going to cry. My dad wouldn't want that. He'd always told me a man's true measure was his strength.

"Chin up, Andrew. You're a Wentworth. We're made of steel."

Today we're having a memorial service for him. My chin will stay up, and my back will stay straight. When I look at the family pictures of my parents and me on a long table at the funeral home and my eyes start to feel watery, I pinch my leg through the pocket of my suit pants. The burning sting in my thigh makes me angry instead of sad.

Better. Dad used to yell at people from his company sometimes, so I know he wouldn't mind me being angry. At night, when I'm staring up at the stars me and Dad stuck on my ceiling when I was little, my stomach twists and hurts with the anger I feel for the men who killed my dad.

They murdered thousands of people. I'm not the only kid without a dad now. Everyone is scared. Nothing will ever be the same.

My mom covers her mouth with her hand, crying as one of her friends squeezes her arm and talks to her. They did that, too. They made my mom cry. My dad wouldn't stand for that.

Since he's gone, I have to be the strong one now. I have to take care of my mom like he would. I have to think about what dad would want for us. I have to hold on tight to my need for those men to pay for what they did to my dad.

The firefighters will eventually extinguish the smoldering fire at Ground Zero, but the fire burning inside of me will never go out.

Chapter One

October 2015

Quinn

THERE'S NOTHING GOOD in Mauricio's Dumpster tonight. Hard pieces of uneaten pizza crust and cold spaghetti covered in olive oil are the only edible things I've found so far. And it won't get better if I dig further. So why am I still ripping open bags of trash on this cold fall evening?

Because my little sister is hungry. I can still see the hope that was shining in her huge blue eyes when I left for a food run earlier. If we've learned only one thing in our four years on the streets of New York City, it's that hunger and cold are realities, but facing them at the same time is a bitch.

I climb up a pile of trash heaped at the end of the rusted Dumpster, bracing my foot on a stack of empty pizza boxes. My hair whips across my face when the chilly breeze catches it.

Fall is my least favorite season now. I loved it when I was a kid and it meant hot, spicy cider, piles of crunchy leaves to plow through, and football games to cheer at.

But now, fall means the dreaded, bitter winter is on its way. I'll spend my days taking Bethy from one heated public place to another in an effort to stay warm. At night, we'll sleep underground. The cold down there isn't life threatening, but some of the people are.

I'm so tired. It hits me all at once, and I sag against a filled plastic trash bag. Last night we got kicked out of the park and chased by a group of frat boys threatening to gang rape Bethy and me. If there hadn't been nine of them, my friend Bean and I would've wiped the cocky grins off their faces.

Fucking rich boys. Their sense of entitlement is staggering.

I sigh and crawl back down the trash hill. The wail of a siren approaches as I fish a plastic bag out of my pocket and stuff the cold spaghetti noodles into it.

It's food, and Bethy won't complain. We've both eaten worse to stave off hunger pangs.

I close my eyes, pushing down the wave of anger welling inside me. The fatigue won't go away if I sleep well tonight. It's bone-deep. I'm tired of running. Tired of feeding my sister scraps of food other people threw away. Tired of wondering if the hell I saved her from is worse than the one I brought her into.

Thinking about this will drain me. I force the thoughts away, wrap my hands around the edge of the Dumpster and swing my leg over.

Two more years. That's what I focus on instead. In a little over two years, Bethy will turn eighteen and we can have a real life. I'll get a job, and she'll go back to school. We'll stop running and looking over our shoulders constantly. We won't go to bed hungry or cold ever again. I'll make sure of it.

The alley is quiet. It's just me and a chubby guy smoking a cigarette, the orange glow of its end bright in the blackness. I put my head down and stuff my hands in the pockets of my coat.

"Hey." The man's voice is deep and insistent. I don't look

up at him.

"Hey, I'm talkin' to you." This time, he grabs my upper arm. I shake myself out of his grasp and push off the ground to run away, but his arm locks around me.

"What's your fuckin' problem?" His warm breath smells like cigarettes and garlic, and I turn away when it hits my face.

I thrash, struggling to escape his hold. He laughs at me.

"Tough girl, huh?"

He's bulky, and I can't stop him from slamming my slight frame against a brick wall. The more I fight, the harder he laughs.

"Let go," I say in a level tone. He presses my upper arms against the cold stone so hard it burns, and he laughs some more.

"You think you're too good for me?"

I kick him in the shin, and he pulls my arms forward and then slams me against the wall again. The impact rattles my teeth and knocks the wind out of me.

And now I'm pissed.

"Please don't hurt me," I say in a tiny voice.

"Scared now, aren't you?" The satisfaction in his tone sends my adrenaline racing. "You better be."

"I'll do whatever you want. Just . . . please don't hurt me." My voice shakes, and he relaxes his grip on me.

It takes me less than a second to knee him in the crotch and wrap my hand around the knife in my leg holster. In a move too fast for this lard-ass to see, let alone block, I pull it out and sink the blade into his gut. Underhanded—harder to block. If I wanted to kill him, I'd pull it out quickly and stab him again with the tight, quick jabs Bean taught me. But he's not worth the trouble.

There's resistance from his flannel and his skin, but once I get past that, it's a smooth trip through layers of fat. My arm muscles tingle as I hold the knife in place for a few seconds.

I see the whites of his eyes get larger. His mouth drops open as he stares at me in disbelief.

"You *bitch,*" he mutters. I'm not gentle when I pull out my knife. He cries out and puts his hands over the wound. I quickly wipe the two sides of my blade on his shirt to clean it.

He reaches for my wrist, but I'm faster. I've landed a punch to his meaty face before he even realizes it's coming.

"Want some more?" I ask, flashing the business end of my blade.

"No." He backs up a few steps, shaking his head.

I arch my brows at him. "Who's scared now?"

I don't wait for an answer. Instead, I turn and head for the street, where sirens are once again wailing in the distance.

My knife tucked safely away once again, I turn my thoughts back to Bethy and Bean. It'll be cold tonight. Much as I hate to do it, it's time for us to head back underground.

Andrew

IT'S POSSIBLY THE worst sales presentation I've ever seen. The guy trying to sell me his software company got Strike One when he didn't introduce himself to me. And now he's tapping his foot on the ground like he's about to piss his pants or something. Strike Two.

"This thing could be *huge*. You know what I'm saying, Mr. Wentworth?" he asks me, grinning.

"Not at all."

His smile slides away, and he clears his throat. "Um, well . . . like I said, I've already made close to a million on it."

"How much have you made? Precisely?"

His Adam's apple bobs as he swallows. "Seven hundred thousand or so . . . sir."

I lower my brows. "Seven hundred twenty-one thousand eleven dollars. That's according to the paperwork your CPA prepared and forwarded to me at your request."

He nods. "Sounds about right."

"About right?" I hold back a sigh of disgust. "This is likely the biggest meeting of your life to date, and you don't have the answer to that critical question prepared?"

"Well, I . . . I knew it was in the papers, so . . ."

"Seven hundred twenty-thousand is *not* close enough to a million to call 'close to a million.' Especially when you subtract your start-up expenses from that figure. Cash flow of this venture is nearly nonexistent at this point."

He silently concedes my point. "It's still got a lot of potential."

I'm about to lay out the cold, hard truth when my secretary, Susan, opens the door.

"Sorry to interrupt, Mr. Wentworth, but Preston McCoy is here and he says it's urgent."

My stomach clenches into a knot of tension as I stand and button my suit coat.

"Go ahead," the nameless man offers, sitting down on the leather sofa in my office. "I'll hang out here."

His suggestion that I'm going to step out of my own office while he "hangs out" here is Strike Three.

"Thank you for your time," I say, heading for the door.

"Oh." His expression is crestfallen. "We're done, then?"

"We're done."

He stacks his poster boards in a pile and packs his laptop into its canvas bag covered with buttons advocating marijuana legalization.

"So . . . when will you know?" he asks.

I meet the gaze of one of my vice presidents, Carla, and I can tell she's holding back a smile.

"I'm not interested in purchasing your company," I say, spelling it out.

"Really?"

Susan puts a hand on his shoulder and steers him from my office before I blow.

"How the hell did he get this meeting?" I ask Carla.

"His mother is a friend of your mother."

I just stare at her for a second. "My *mother* set this up?"

"Well . . . she asked if you'd donate to the hospital league banquet, and then she told Susan she'd accept an hour of your time in place of the monetary donation."

My mother only accepts the word *no* when someone is saying, "No problem, Mrs. Wentworth." I learned much of my tenacity from her, but I can't have her using my time this way. I make a mental note to discuss this with her.

Preston McCoy steps into my office, his gray comb-over sparser than the last time I saw him.

"Andrew. Carla." He shakes both our hands, and Carla steps out. Preston's gaze stays fixed on her ass as she departs. The old perv isn't even sly about it.

"So," he says, sitting down in one of the leather wingback chairs in front of my desk.

I hold up a hand to stop him, walk over to my office door, and close it. Susan generally makes sure my door is closed for meetings, but she's probably still getting rid of the pot proponent.

Preston waits for me to unbutton my jacket and sit down. I meet his gaze, not letting on that my stomach is churning, ready to spill its contents. I know why he's here. He has the answer I've been waiting seven long months for.

"The paternity test results are in, and you are in no way related to Ms. Henley's child."

My insides liquefy with relief. *Thank fuck.* I press my

sweating palms to my thighs and wait for Preston to continue.

"Ms. Henley has dropped her claim for child support. It's over, Andrew."

I nod. "Good. Thank you for coming by with the news."

"Of course. I can file a claim for the ten thousand a month you provided as support during the pregnancy."

I can still see Amber Henley's quaking lower lip when she told me in my kitchen that our one and only sexual encounter had gotten her pregnant, and there was no doubt I was the father of the baby she was carrying. The bottom of my world fell out that day. At age twenty-eight, I was just hitting my stride with my company. Not to mention she wasn't someone I saw myself with long-term.

I'd royally fucked that kid over before it was even born. Wasn't in love with its mother and wasn't ready to be a father. I'd spent a lot of the past seven months loathing myself over it.

And after all that, Amber had been lying. I can't even be angry about it because the relief overpowers everything else.

"I don't care about the money," I tell Preston. "Like you said, it's over."

He arches his brows in a judgmental glare. "Well, maybe this'll be a lesson to you."

"I'm not paying you a thousand an hour for life lessons," I say, my tone crisp. "Now if you'll excuse me."

"Of course. I apologize." He gets up and leaves my office, closing the door behind him.

I turn my desk chair toward the window and look out at the expanse of stone on the building next door.

It's over. I didn't wrong my unborn child. I don't have to deal with gold-digging Amber anymore. If I ever cried, I'd weep with relief right now.

Instead, I sigh deeply and run a hand over the light five-o'clock shadow coating my cheeks.

Never again will I cede control of my life to a woman this way. I won't give Preston the satisfaction of admitting this *was* a lesson to me. From now on, I hold all the cards.

Chapter Two

Quinn

I'D FORGOTTEN HOW dark it was in the tunnels. It's the kind of pitch blackness where you can't even see your hand in front of your face. I hear the sounds of Bethy and Bean breathing beside me and the faint rumble of people talking ahead of us.

"I hate this place," Bethy says, her low tone nearly a whisper.

"Better than freezing," I remind her.

"I guess."

The gurgle of a hunger pang from her stomach makes me press my lips together in a thin line. We haven't had a full meal in nearly a week. Just bits and pieces of what we can dig up here and there. The only soup kitchen I'm comfortable going to is in a very seedy neighborhood about seven miles away. That's a long walk in the cold, especially when Bethy has a hole in the bottom of one of her shoes.

"You guys won't leave me down here by myself, right?" Bethy's voice wobbles with nervousness.

"Never. One of us always stays with you."

"Just . . . making sure."

"Hey." Bean's gravelly tone commands attention. "We ain't never let nothin' happen to you, girl. Nothin' to worry about."

I'd be lost without him. Bean has become a most unlikely ally. When he crept up on us in these abandoned subway tunnels two years ago, I thought for sure he was going to slit my throat and make off with my sister. His dark eyes were menacing even in the dim light of the flashlight he'd pointed at us. I'd been too incapacitated with pneumonia to even react.

But he'd surprised me and helped us. I'll never forget it. Now we're a threesome. Me, my kid sister, and a thirty-six-year-old Mexican man with a wicked scar across his cheek and only one hand.

But Bean can take care of business with the hand he has left. I trust him with Bethy. Without him, I don't know if we'd still be here. Even with his help, in dark moments I've considered surrendering to the people who are looking for Bethy and me.

No.

Every time that thought creeps in, I dig deep and find the strength to keep going. We've been living this life for four and a half years. What's two more?

Bethy coughs and I stiffen. That hacking sound is one of the reasons I decided to come back down to the tunnels at night. Bethy's sick, and we can't keep sleeping outside in this weather.

The glow of a lantern ahead illuminates the forms of around a dozen people. My hand instinctively lowers to the knife strapped to my thigh.

"Me first," Bean says when we're close enough that people start turning to look at us. He pushes his way through the group and into the darkened alcove where we'll sleep tonight.

It smells like pot smoke and vomit. But the icy wind isn't cutting into my skin like it does outside. I'll make that trade.

Bethy shrugs off the sleeping bag strapped to her back, and I help her spread it out. Her eyes meet mine as she crawls inside, and even in the dim light of the nearby lantern I see the question there.

Are we eating tonight?

She won't ask me out loud. She learned a long time ago that asking just reminds us how hungry we are. I kind of wish she would ask me, though. I wish she'd give me a dirty look and say she hates me for taking away her warm bed and full stomach at home in exchange for this.

The guilt eats me up. I wish she'd confront me about this miserable existence. I wouldn't even try to defend myself at this point.

But she won't. She trusts me completely. She keeps me up when I get down. And that makes it so much worse when I fail her.

"I'll go up for food," I say. Her eyes light hopefully.

"I got it," Bean says, zipping up his worn canvas coat.

"You sure?"

He takes a small handgun from his pocket and passes it to me.

"Take my gun," he says loudly. "It's loaded."

Several heads swivel in our direction. Bean just protected us with his words. I take the weapon and nod.

His boots crunch against the shards of gravel on the ground as he heads away from the tunnel. I sit with my back to Bethy, the gun in my lap. Its presence will scare off most people who'd consider jumping us, but others are crazy and desperate enough to jump me in an attempt to steal the gun.

I hope Bean comes through with food. Between a decent meal and some rest, Bethy might be feeling better tomorrow.

A man with a long beard and wild eyes studies me from twenty feet away. I cock the gun and point it at him. He turns away, and I lower it back to my lap, sighing.

Sometimes surviving is exhausting.

BETHY IS COUGHING so hard she has to stop walking. She bends over and takes a few deep breaths, but she immediately starts coughing again right after.

Bean locks eyes with me for an instant. He's worried. I am, too. I'm about out of my mind with worry. It's been three days since we started sleeping in the tunnel, and Bethy's cough has only gotten worse.

"It's okay," I say, placing a hand on her back.

But it's not. She needs rest and food, and maybe medicine, too. We have to clear out of the tunnels at sunrise every morning. That's an unwritten rule of sleeping down there. If we get busted, we'll all lose out, so we only stay there when it's dark.

"I hear there's a free clinic downtown," Bean says.

"No."

His eyes narrow slightly, but he doesn't press me. Bean doesn't know why I refuse to go anywhere that requires ID, but he knows I'm adamant about it.

Bethy stands back up, squares her shoulders and gives us a weak smile. Her eyes are red-rimmed, and her collarbone has become more prominent. A knot of tension forms in my stomach.

"She can give 'em a fake name," Bean mumbles.

"No," I say sharply. "I have another plan."

His brows shoot up in question. The doubt in his expression forces my gaze to Bethy, who is still smiling at me. Unlike Bean, she trusts that I've got this situation covered. I can't take either thing—his doubt or her certainty. My chest is tight with the pressure of it.

"Give me an hour," I say to Bean. "You guys meet me back

here then."

He gives me a slight nod and turns to my sister. "You okay to walk over to the subway entrance? We can warm up in there."

"Sure." She coughs again and then takes the arm he's holding out to support her.

Bean is pissed at me, and I can't even blame him. Bethy is suffering out here. Not only is she sick, cold, and hungry, she's missed the last four-and-a-half years of school. She'll be eighteen in two years, and I'll be twenty-three. I was sixteen when we came here, and I just recently turned twenty-one. But what options will either of us have without even a high school diploma?

The tightness in my chest is getting painful. It's too much, worrying about this right now. I have to focus on getting Bethy better. And with nothing but the clothes on my back and forty-four cents in my backpack pocket, I have no idea how to do that.

A pain shoots through my stomach, distinctive from the one in my chest. It's a hunger pang. Hunger is such a constant I don't think about it much anymore, but sometimes my body forces me to.

People are walking around me as I stand motionless on the sidewalk. I'm used to the contemptuous glares and dismissive head shakes. It's obvious I'm homeless. I smell and I'm wearing rags. But still, I want to scream at these people that I'm still a person. I used to be like them—concerned about whether I'd be able to find a shirt to match a new skirt or completely absorbed in a text conversation about nothing at all.

There's a small niche carved out of a tall building, and I head for it, needing to escape the crowd. I just lean against the wall for a minute, taking a few deep breaths. Then I let my back slide down the brick wall, its surface scratching my skin through the thin fabric of my coat. When I'm sitting on the ground, I pull my legs up to my chest and wrap my arms around them, resting my chin atop my knees. For just a minute, I can sit here and admit to myself that things are bad. Worse than they've been since we got here. Since I'm alone and there's no one to be strong for, I can give in to the drowning helplessness.

A woman tosses a half-eaten sandwich into a metal trash can near the curb, and I cringe. Why? Why the hell do some people have enough to mindlessly toss food in the trash while others physically ache from hunger?

I'm haunted by the food I threw away when I was younger. If our cook put peppers in the spaghetti sauce, I'd refused to eat it. If she accidentally put mayo on my sandwich, it went straight into the trash can in the school cafeteria.

What I wouldn't give for some of Lydia's spaghetti with peppers in the sauce right now. I'd eat until my stomach was about to burst and force Bethy to do the same. There's an insecurity to this life that makes me hold on tightly to what little I do have. And all I have is my sister. That's why her cough scares me so much.

I press my forehead to my knees, willing myself to keep calm. There's always a way. Sometimes I have to do things I never imagined doing, but we're still standing, so it's worth it.

I'll have to steal. The streets have taught me to be stealthy, and I can lift a wallet without being noticed as long as I have time to wait for the right mark.

Time isn't on my side today, though. I have forty-five minutes until Bethy and Bean will be back. I'll have to work fast.

"Excuse me."

I look up at the source of the warm male voice that pulled me from my thoughts. He's a little taller than average, with a lean physique and short black hair styled in a neat faux-hawk. His cashmere scarf and expensive-looking wool coat make me wish he wouldn't have noticed me, because this guy would have made a great mark.

"What?" I ask, my voice flat and lifeless. "I'm not trespassing. This is public property."

His lips curve into a slight smile. "I just wanted to ask if you'd like to get a cup of coffee. Maybe some breakfast? You look like you could use a break."

My brow furrows as I stare up at him. "And why would you give me a break?"

He shrugs. "Someone gave me a break once."

My stomach begs me to say yes. I stand up and meet the man's brown eyes. "I've got no money. You're offering to buy?"

"I am."

"And what do I have to give you for it?"

"Nothing. We'll talk and eat and then go our separate ways if you'd like. No hard feelings."

"I'm *not* blowing you or letting you bend me over a Dumpster somewhere," I say in an even, no-nonsense tone.

He cringes. *Cringes.* Do I smell that bad?

"Ah . . . I'm not interested in that," he says with a shake of his head.

I shrug a shoulder and nod at a diner across the street. "Over there?"

"Sure." He pulls a dark glove from a well-manicured hand and offers it to me. "I'm Dawson Wright, by the way."

I give him a perfunctory handshake. "So let's go, Dawson."

He's still looking at me. "And your name is . . . ?"

I scoff. "Does it matter?"

"Why wouldn't it?" His brow wrinkles in confusion.

"Most people don't even see me, let alone care what my name is. I'm about as important as the dirt on the bottom of their shoes."

"I'm not most people. What's your name?"

I'm taken aback, but I don't show it. "Quinn."

He nods, satisfied, and leads the way across the street and into a packed diner. As soon as I step inside, the smells of bacon, toasting bread, and cinnamon hit me hard. My stomach rumbles painfully. It's been a long time since I set foot in a place like this.

A passing waitress gives me the evil eye as we walk to a tiny booth next to the windows facing the street. I bristle, preparing myself to get kicked out of the place. She returns to our table and sees Dawson. Her expression morphs into a smile.

"What can I get you two?" she asks.

I glance at a menu while Dawson orders coffee. The waitress looks at me expectantly.

"Coffee and a house omelet with two side orders of bacon and two side orders of toast. And some oatmeal in a takeout container."

Dawson doesn't blink at my large order. The waitress disappears, and he leans his forearms on the table and studies me.

"So what's your story, Quinn?"

I arch a brow. "It's a little early in the day for life stories, isn't it?"

"I suppose," he says, smiling. "I know you seem to have the weight of the world on your shoulders. And you really like bacon."

Our waitress reappears and fills the empty white mugs in front of us with steaming coffee. I sip it gratefully. I haven't had hot coffee in a while. There's something soothing about it. I savor another swallow as the waitress walks away.

"So," Dawson says, clearing his throat. "I know this seems sudden, but I have a proposition. I'd like to buy an evening with you."

I sip my coffee and try to decide how to play this. I can't risk pissing him off and not getting that food. I decide to buy some time with the *tell me more* approach.

"An evening?"

He nods. "You'd need to submit to a quick blood draw from a nurse first. It's a standard screen. And then you'd spend a mutually enjoyable evening having consensual sex with a man I think you'd like."

I set my mug down, curiosity piqued. "Not you?"

"No, not me. My boss."

"Oh."

His wry smile is back. "If I liked spending evenings with women, I'm sure I'd love one with you. But I've got a boyfriend."

I nod. "I see. Well, I appreciate the offer, but I'll need to—"

"The pay is five hundred dollars up front."

His words stop me cold.

Five.

Hundred.

Dollars.

That's more than I can steal. Enough to take Bethy to a doctor and buy food for the next month or more.

And money up front? I could climb out a bathroom window before the guy even got my pants off.

"And you think your boss would like me? Is he into homeless women? Or . . . *wait*. Do you think I'm a prostitute?"

The thought sends a wave of unease through me. Why, I'm not sure, because it's not like I have much pride left.

"No. My employer specifically doesn't like that kind of thing."

"What kinds of things *does* he like?"

The waitress delivers the food to our table, arranging five plates in front of me. I dive into the omelet as Dawson responds.

"He'd like you. I know that. I'd put you up in a hotel for an afternoon so you could get ready, and I'd provide clothes for you."

The wheels in my mind are spinning as I try to stop and actually taste the hot, cheesy eggs melting in my mouth. The food is so good, but I'm devouring it.

"I'd get the room for the whole night?"

"Well, you'd be at his place that night."

"I know, but . . . for my friend. She could sleep there while I was . . . you know."

"Sure, that wouldn't be a problem."

This is too good to pass up. I pull napkins from a dispenser and wrap the bacon and toast in them as I mull the idea of Bethy and Bean warm in a hotel for a night. And fed for the next few weeks.

It's unexpected, but this is the break I've been waiting for. Taking money to have sex with a strange man in his home makes me more than uneasy, but I'll have to work around it.

"I'm not very experienced," I confess to Dawson. "And I wouldn't give back any of the money just because he wasn't happy with me."

"He'll like you. I'm certain of it."

I nod slightly. "I'll need the money in cash. And I want some sort of ID from this nurse you mentioned. No one's sticking a needle in me if I'm not sure they're a nurse."

"Understandable."

I meet his eyes across the table. "And I get to keep my knife on me."

Dawson's lips part slightly. "Well . . . weapons might kill the mood, don't you think?"

"I keep my knife. That's nonnegotiable. And you can let your boss know I'm damned good with it."

He hesitates for a second. "Okay. If that makes you more comfortable."

I pack the bacon and toast into my backpack and wrap my hands around the cardboard bowl of oatmeal I'm taking.

"*One guy*," I say adamantly. "No gang bang. No one watching. No creepy videotaping."

"Of course not. My employer wants this to be a mutually enjoyable night."

"He does this all the time, then?"

A smile plays on Dawson's lips. "I wouldn't say that, but you aren't the first."

"How ugly is he, between you and me? Are we talking open sores or anything? Just so I know."

"No." Dawson laughs but quickly regains his composure. "He's actually very attractive."

"Hmm," I grunt skeptically.

Must have a small dick, then.

A glance at the clock tells me I need to go. "I'll expect protection. Condoms, I mean."

"Of course."

"Okay, then. I guess I'm in. But I can change my mind and refund the money if I get there and see a sex dungeon or something."

"Excellent. There's no dungeon."

Dawson pulls out a small notebook and writes down the name and address of a hotel. "Tomorrow. Come by at noon. That gives us time to get the blood work done and have you ready for the evening."

I nod and slide out of my side of the booth. "See you then. Thanks for the food."

"See you tomorrow, Quinn."

As I make my way to the door of the densely packed diner, I realize it's been a while since anyone but Bethy or Bean used my name. To most people, I don't even have a name. I'm just a statistic.

I never foresaw this being my life. Homelessness wasn't even on my radar before I took Bethy and ran. And now I've sunk a little lower yet, selling my body.

Well, promising to sell it, anyway. But that's one promise

I'm planning to wiggle out of. I'm hoping this mystery guy will settle for a blow job. The last thing I want him finding out is that his paid companion is actually a virgin.

Chapter Three

Andrew

A CLOUD OF breath forms in front of my face as I step out of my car in my underground garage. Winter is setting in fast, and in typical New York style, it refuses to be ignored.

I press my thumb to the keypad beside the elevator in my garage and step on, arriving at the main level of my warehouse home and hearing the *thunk* of the automated deadbolt opening. When I step inside, I take in the scent of roasting beef. Damn, that smells good. It's a little after six thirty, and I'm ready for dinner.

But not because of the food. I'm sure I'll enjoy whatever delicacy my chef and housekeeper, Turner, has cooking right now, but mostly I'm eager to spend an evening with Dawson's latest find. For a gay man, he really does have incredible taste in women.

I can't be seen trying to pick up women I intend to pay for sex. And I don't have time to screw with it, anyway. That's why I have Dawson. He earns every penny of the six figures I pay him to be my personal assistant. I trust him implicitly, which is no small thing for me.

Last weekend he brought me Olivia, who nearly swallowed my cock as she worked to prove how deep she could take it. She screamed my name like a porn star when she came, and I knew her performance was an effort to get a return invitation.

But I don't give return invitations.

I shrug off my suit jacket and lay it over the back of a chair. Everything looks to be in order as I glance around the open rooms of my home. A faint lemon scent and a shine on my hardwood floors tell me Turner was hard at work here today.

After a long day of negotiations to purchase a new technology app, I need to unwind. I made a fair offer, but the snotty college kid I'm trying to buy from is greedy. And as much as I want that app, I refuse to pay more for it, even if it means losing it to someone else.

I pull off my navy blue tie and unfasten the top button of my shirt. I'm heading to my bedroom with the tie when a knock at the front door makes me turn. After tossing the tie on my leather sofa, I walk to the wide, solid wood door and press my thumb to a keypad beside it to open it. The deadbolt slides free, and I open the door.

For a split second, I make out Dawson. But my attention is quickly and entirely focused on the woman beside him.

Fuck yes. She's exactly what I need. Average height, with a slim frame and blond, shoulder-length hair. Her creamy complexion is tinged pink from the cold, matching her beautiful, full lips. She studies me back with huge hazel eyes, and I pick up on her discomfort.

"Hi. Come on inside," I say, stepping back from the door.

"What is this place?" she mumbles as she follows Dawson in. Her hand rests on her thigh beneath a dark coat that looks new.

"It's a bit off-putting, I know," I say. "But I love the

Meatpacking District."

"You *live* here?" Her gaze moves around the massive, open two stories of my living room and kitchen.

"I do."

Dawson steps in. "Andrew, this is Quinn. Quinn, Andrew."

I extend my hand to Quinn, and she hesitates a second before shaking it briefly. She tilts her face up to look at me, and I wonder what she's trying to determine. Perhaps she's taken aback by my size. At six foot two, I'm much taller than her, and my broad shoulders match my height. I've got a good fifty pounds on Dawson.

"Nice to meet you," I say.

Her skeptical gaze tells me she's not sure how nice it is just yet. I'll change that.

"I'm off, then," Dawson says, locking eyes with me. "Everything's in order."

I give him a curt nod of approval. So Quinn's blood work came back clean and she's been paid. Now all that's left is to shake off this long day in bed with her. After I loosen her up over dinner, of course.

Dawson slips out, and Quinn eyes me warily. She must be nervous.

"Can I take your coat?" I offer.

She shrugs off the coat, revealing a simple black V-neck shirt and dark gray linen pants. I can't help letting my gaze slide over the lines of her. She's stunning. My big hands will almost span her entire slender waistline. The definition in her collarbone is begging to be kissed and tasted at length.

"I refused to wear any of those dresses Dawson brought to me," she explains. "I'm not a hooker."

I hold back the smile quirking on my lips. I like her, and I'm not about to argue about whether wearing a dress or accepting money for sex makes a woman a hooker.

"You look beautiful," I say instead. "If you're hungry, we can have some dinner."

She nods and turns toward the kitchen. I finally see what her hand is resting on, and I can't help reacting.

"What the hell . . . ? Is that a *hunting knife*?"

Her gaze snaps back to me. "I told Dawson I'm keeping it. He said it's okay."

My heart stirs to life in my chest. Is she scared of me? Doesn't she realize she doesn't stand a chance against me with that thing?

"Well . . ." I rub my chin and consider how to put her at ease. "You won't need that. I'm only into consensual sex."

"All the same, I prefer to keep it."

There's a harshness to her eyes now. I wonder what made this beautiful woman feel the need to strap a knife to her thigh and be ready to draw it at a moment's notice. Fucking humanity. It's why I live in this warehouse with multiple layers of security. It's nondescript on the outside so as not to attract attention. I'm not a flashy penthouse kind of guy. I prefer to wield power in stealthier ways.

"Of course," I say, leading the way into the kitchen. Quinn follows soundlessly.

"Would you like some wine?" I ask.

"No thanks. I'll have some water, though."

I pour her half a glass of red wine and a glass full of Perrier and set both in front of her. I won't push the wine on her, but clearly she could use a few sips to ease her nerves.

The glass of wine I pour myself smells of apples and peppers. I take a slow sip, lean back against the butcher block kitchen island and let my gaze roam the gorgeous, guarded woman standing before me.

"So tell me about yourself, Quinn."

She shrugs. "Not much to tell. I'm homeless, but I guess

you know that."

"I didn't. I'm sorry."

"I wasn't looking for your pity. I just figured all the women Dawson picks up for you are homeless."

The edge in her tone pisses me off. Not just because no one talks to me this way, but also because of her innuendo.

"You're suggesting I prey on desperate women?" I ask coolly.

She shrugs. "Is it preying if they take your offer?"

"*Dawson's* offer."

"Of course. Your hands are clean."

I clear my throat and remind myself to keep cool. None of the women Dawson's brought over before has arrived with an enormous chip on her shoulder. To the contrary, they've been giddy with excitement.

"Look, Quinn, if you don't want to be here, you're free to go. Keep the money."

She bristles visibly, her eyes narrowing. "No, I made a deal, and I'll keep it. But I don't think we have much in common. Conversation will just be awkward. Maybe we should just get to it."

I arch my brows in amusement. She can't seriously think I'm hard right now. "Get to . . . ?"

Her cheeks flush. "Eating. And then . . . whatever. Look, I feel like I should tell you I'm really inexperienced. Maybe I should have told Dawson that. I'm hoping a blow job will be . . . enough."

I can't hold back a small smile. There's something about Quinn's tough façade I find incredibly vulnerable.

"Hey," I say softly. "Relax. Let's just have some dinner and talk."

"You're not paying five hundred bucks for my conversational skills."

I look up at the ceiling. This is like trying to seduce a cactus, her prickly points jabbing me at every turn. "That may be true, but . . . I'm not going to force myself on you."

Her expression is skeptical. I reach for the buttons on my dress shirt cuffs and unfasten them, rolling my sleeves up slowly. I like the way she watches me, her gaze wandering over my forearms.

I can command anything. My father taught me that. Control doesn't have to be an unpleasant experience for either party. If I want to relax Quinn and make her smile, I will.

"Sit down," I say softly. "I'm going to make you a plate of dinner. We're going to eat and talk. You're *not* going to stab me. Okay?"

She nods, the wariness seemingly dissipating, and sinks into one of the wood chairs at my kitchen table.

"This place is amazing," she says softly. "I've seen a lot of fancy houses, but none of them compare to this."

"Thank you. I oversaw the renovation myself. It's got an industrial style, so I think it's just the size that makes it seem luxurious."

I pull the roasted beef from a warming oven, slice it, and put generous portions on two plates. After adding roasted red potatoes and sautéed asparagus, I carry the plates to the table and set one in front of Quinn.

"Wow." She looks up at me. "This looks delicious. You made this?"

I shake my head, wishing for a second that I had. "No, I've got someone who cooks for me."

She looks down at the food, her eyes swimming with emotion. I'm trying to figure out what's going on. Is she upset? She presses her lips together, and finally, I get it.

She's hungry. The thought sends a burning sensation to my chest.

"Let's eat," I say, sitting down quickly.

Quinn's utter satisfaction upon tasting the first bite of beef is something I won't soon forget. Her expression relaxes as she chews and cuts another bite.

I'm eating, too, but all I can think about is feeding this woman. The lithe frame I find so sexy—is it a result of not having enough to eat? The thought makes me feel like a callous asshole.

"Do you like it?" I ask.

She nods. "It's delicious. Thank you."

I wait until she's eaten more than half the food on her plate to interrupt her with conversation again.

"Can I ask how you found yourself on the streets?" I ask. "You don't seem like the type to end up there."

"Lots of decent people are homeless," she says with a touch of defensiveness.

I'm silent as she takes a bite of potatoes, studying me. Is she sizing me up, or is she attracted to me? I can usually read people better than I'm reading her right now.

"It was just . . . circumstance," she finally says. "I needed to get away from someone. It's easy to be invisible on the streets here."

"How old were you? How old are you now?"

"I was sixteen when I got here, and I'm twenty-one now."

She cuts her asparagus carefully. "How did you get so rich? How old are you?"

"I'm twenty-eight. I capitalize companies for ownership interest and buy others outright."

She nods as she finishes her last bite of food.

"More?" I ask, reaching for the plate.

"I'm full, but thanks."

Her expression shifts back to nervousness, and she reaches for the wine and takes a tiny sip. I can't help laughing at her cringe.

"Don't like it?"

She shakes her head. "It's not what I was expecting."

"It's an acquired taste."

I clear away the dishes as she downs a few gulps of water.

"So," she says, standing up, "I'm really curious about why you pay women to be with you. You're rich and not unattractive. Lots of women would kill to be with you for free."

"Nothing's free. It's not me they want, it's the money. I prefer to be upfront about my intentions."

"And your intentions are . . . ?" She looks me over, and I like the interest I see in her pretty hazel eyes.

"Sex. I'm not looking to be tied down. Companionship is good, but I don't like expectations."

She nods with understanding. "I can see that. And your work must keep you busy."

"It does."

I leave the dishes on the counter for Turner to see to tomorrow. Quinn is leaning against my large kitchen island, and I approach her, my blood pumping harder with every step.

"You are exceptionally beautiful," I say, feeling a little like a high school kid with a crush.

She smiles, her perfect white teeth adding to her mystery. At some point, she obviously had braces and the best of dental care. It's not just that, though. It's also the set of her shoulders and the way she fearlessly holds my gaze. She could be wearing rags, and she'd still have an air of class.

"Thanks," she says. "It's just the hair and makeup Dawson's stylist did for me."

I step closer, shaking my head. "I have a feeling you'd be just as perfect straight out of the shower," I say in a low tone. When I reach for her jawline and run my thumb across it, her eyes flutter closed for a split second.

I let my fingertips graze over the creamy skin of her long neck, brushing past her soft, golden waves. Her eyes open wide and she stiffens.

"What?" I ask softly, pulling my hand away. "You don't like that?"

She swallows and looks up into my eyes. "It's hard. This is . . . harder than I thought it would be."

I step back, and she bites her lower lip and furrows her brow.

"My instinct is to react like you're going to choke me," she admits. "No one ever touches me there. Or anywhere. Except . . . one person. I only let one person touch me."

A cloud of jealousy darkens over my field of vision. Who is this person who touches her, and how is he deserving? Clearly he doesn't take care of her.

"You have a boyfriend," I say, surprised by how much that disappoints me.

"No. I didn't mean someone like that. It's . . . my sibling."

"Oh."

I fold my arms over my chest and lean against the island next to her.

"Sorry," she says softly. "I know I'm not doing this right."

"Tell me more about your sibling," I say. "Brother or sister?"

"I can't." She turns to face me, tilting her face up until our eyes meet. The swirl of gold and green and brown in her eyes is mesmerizing. "I might feel more comfortable if . . . instead of you touching me first, can I touch you?"

My lips part for just a second at the question. I feel a primal urge to reach for her hands and put them on me, to tell her that *fuck yes, she can touch me.* Anywhere. Everywhere. I want those slender fingers to explore the body I spend so much time honing in the gym.

But instead, I just nod, trying my best not to scare her off. I don't even mind this excruciatingly slow seduction. In fact, I'm fully erect in my suit pants right now.

There are secrets in the depths of her eyes. I see pain and vulnerability there, laced with a strength that turns me on hard. Tonight, I get to show this intriguing, incredibly sexy woman that not everyone wants to hurt her.

Chapter Four

Quinn

I REACH OUT tentatively, my eyes locked on Andrew as my palm meets his chest. The soft fabric of his shirt covers a taut, muscled chest. My fingers trail up and down, sliding over ridges of muscle.

He's strong. Fit. Masculine. All the things most twenty-one-year-old women find sexy in a man. And while I notice all this, am I turned on right now? Do I want him to whisk me off to the bedroom and rock my world?

No.

I'm out of my element, wearing these designer clothes and smelling like expensive perfume. How did I fall so low I'm selling my body to a stranger? What would my mom say if she could see me right now?

And Bethy. I'm worried sick about my sister. It's some comfort that she's warm and safe in a hotel room right now, but she's still sick, and I'm not with her. We rarely leave each other's side. And in the four-and-a-half years we've been on the streets, I've never spent a night apart from her.

Bean will take care of her. I know this. But still, I find it as impossible as ever to think about sex right now. Like so many other things, it's a luxury that's not part of my world.

"You look tense," Andrew says. His voice, like the rest of him, is all man. It's deep and commanding.

I shrug, sliding my hand from his abs around to his waist. "I'm fine."

"When you said you're inexperienced, how inexperienced did you mean?"

I pull my hand away and sigh deeply. "That's kind of personal. I'm not asking for *your* full sexual history or anything."

His brows arch slightly. "I'll tell you anything you want to know. I'm not trying to pry, but I don't want to make you uncomfortable later. You're not a virgin, are you?"

"So what if I am?"

He exhales his frustration through his nose. "Okay . . . well, I need to know what you're comfortable with."

I consider, still looking into his dark blue eyes. "Kissing. Touching . . . and blow jobs."

The corners of his lips curl slightly. He's trying not to laugh, I can tell.

"Look," I say defensively. "Can we just do this? I'm ready."

"I'm not laughing at you, Quinn," he says, his expression turning serious. "It's just that I can see how uncomfortable you are. Maybe this isn't meant to be." His eyes light up with an epiphany. "Hey, are you . . . *definitely* straight? If you're not attracted to men, that would explain this."

I roll my eyes. "Yes, I'm attracted to men. I'm just not attracted to pretentious, arrogant ones."

His amusement is back. "Me, arrogant?"

"Yes, *you*. Like the only way a woman wouldn't want to screw you is because she's gay. Look up arrogance in the dictionary, and you'll see a picture of yourself with that shit-eating grin on your face."

"Is arrogance before or after *uptight* in the dictionary?"

My hand instinctively wraps around the smooth handle of my knife. "Did you seriously just say that to me? Your game needs some serious work."

"My game's never been a problem with other women."

"Other women are probably impressed by your money and swagger. I've lived a privileged life before. It's not all it's cracked up to be."

I hold his gaze, my chin tilted up, as I wait for his next comeback. But instead, he just studies me silently.

"Tell me what you want," he finally says.

I want him to stop looking at me that way. Like what I want matters. Like this is a regular date or something. I want his leather and cologne scent not to smell so damn good. I want his eyes to be less blue and his shoulders not so broad. A man with nearly a foot and probably a hundred pounds on me should have me feeling more cautious than I do right now.

"I want to do whatever I need to so you're . . . satisfied and I can leave."

"Satisfied?" He pauses, his eyes still on mine, and I'm wondering how he can communicate such intensity without words. "I'm very intrigued by you, Quinn. What would satisfy me is to learn more about you over a bottle of good wine."

"The deal was sex."

He nods. "If you'd prefer that, let's get started." He reaches for his belt buckle and unfastens it, pulling on one end until it quickly snakes all the way through the loops on his pants. "Go ahead and get undressed and lay down on the couch. Legs spread. And hold on to your ankles."

I swallow hard. Damn, this is harder than I thought it would be. Neither sex nor sharing personal information appeals to me at the moment.

"Fine," I concede. "Okay. We'll talk, and I'll try to choke

down some wine."

My surly tone makes him smile slightly. "What would you prefer?"

"Something hot would be good. Coffee or tea."

"Are you cold?"

I shake my head, too proud to tell him a hot drink is a rare treat for me. I mostly drink water from public drinking fountains.

"Chai tea," he says, walking over to a high kitchen cabinet and opening it.

I study his back as he does. He's exceptionally tall and broad—I dread running into men his size in the tunnels. They hit hard and are usually impossibly strong. I learned quickly it's best to evade men that big rather than fight them.

"How tall are you?" I ask, sliding into a chair at his square, wood kitchen table.

"Six two."

"Tall parents?"

He nods slightly as he pulls a stainless tea kettle from a cabinet. "My dad was six three."

"Was? How long has he been gone?"

"I was thirteen when he died."

He's looking down at the kettle as he fills it at the kitchen sink, but I can hear from the tension in his voice that the wound still feels raw for him. Something in me softens because never would I have imagined that I had anything in common with a man like him, but I do.

"I'm sorry," I say. "My dad died when I was thirteen."

He meets my gaze from across the room. "I'm sorry. What happened?"

"He had stomach cancer." I shake my head sadly at the memories. "It was awful. What about your dad?"

"9/11."

"Oh." My heart goes out to Andrew in a new way. "So you never got to say good-bye?"

His lips set in a tense line. "No. Not even a real funeral. His remains were never identified."

"That's terrible. I'm so sorry."

Andrew shrugs and switches on the gas burner of his wide, stainless range, setting the tea kettle on it. "It's been fourteen years now. I'm fine."

"I'm not," I admit. "I miss my dad so much it hurts. Every day."

"What about your mom? Is she still around?"

I blow out a breath. "As far as I know."

"Not close to your mom, I take it. Where did you live before you found yourself on the streets?"

"I can't talk about that."

His brow furrows. "You can't? Or won't?"

"Won't," I concede.

"Okay. Well, how about the sibling you mentioned earlier? Brother or sister? Older or younger?"

I shake my head. "Let's talk about something else."

"Favorite kind of sandwich?"

I smile at the glimmer in his dark blue eyes. "Grilled cheese. You?"

"Pastrami on rye."

"My turn. How many women have you done this with?"

"Talked about my favorite sandwich, you mean?" His tone is light as he gets up to retrieve the kettle from the stovetop.

"Ha-ha. Paid for sex."

He's quiet for a few seconds.

"Too personal?" I ask.

He turns to look at me. "No. I'm adding it up. It's . . . twelve, I think."

"Wow. And you don't worry about knocking someone up

or catching something?"

"Not at all. The blood test, remember?"

I nod. "Right. And I assume you wear condoms."

Andrew clears his throat as he walks to his stainless refrigerator, which is at least eight feet wide. "Ah . . . yes."

"What was that?" I ask.

"What was what?"

"You're hiding something. What is it?"

I see him smiling as he pours splashes of milk into the mugs with tea bags and hot water. He stirs in some sugar and sets the tea bags in an empty mug. I can smell the sweet cinnamon aroma of the drink as he carries it over.

"I'll tell you if you really want to know," he says.

"I do." I pick up the mug and take a test sip. The hot, spicy, sweet tea warms me all over as it slides down my throat. "That's really good."

He nods slightly in acknowledgment of the compliment before speaking. "I usually only have . . . particular kinds of sex."

I set the mug down, eyes wide with surprise. "Oh . . . I see. So oral and . . . ?"

He smiles sheepishly. "Yes."

"Oh, shit," I say softly. "That's . . . never happening with me."

Andrew shrugs. "We all have our kinks, Quinn."

"Is that yours?" I wrap my hands around the mug and grip it.

"I like sex in all its forms. And some women like it, too. It also tends to be less emotional for them, which is a plus."

"Ugh." I cringe. "I wouldn't do that for any amount of money. I'd rather starve."

Now he's the one cringing. I straighten my spine, reminded that he and I are from two different worlds.

"Have you ever thought about getting help?" he asks. "Why

don't you go to shelters or soup kitchens?"

I bristle defensively. "I have my reasons. We get by. I don't need your pity."

"Who is *we*?"

I meet his eyes and shake my head silently.

"You and your sibling? Is there anyone else?" His tone is laced with aggravation.

"It's none of your business."

"Is there a man? A boyfriend? A friend who keeps you warm at night? Anyone?"

"What do you care?"

His gaze is steely now. "I'm just curious."

"For a man who likes anonymous sex, you ask a lot of personal questions."

"Have you ever had oral sex, Quinn?"

"I blew a guy in the tunnels two years ago for twenty bucks. Does that count?"

"Sure."

"Thinking you overpaid me now?"

He shakes his head. "I'm just curious about what you've done before."

I can't help a slight snort of amusement. "Andrew, you really don't get it. Having that old guy's dick in my mouth two years ago is my full sexual resume. I've never even kissed a man. My entire life is about finding the next meal and a safe place to sleep. And usually, I don't look like this. I wear old clothes that don't fit, and I smell. You think guys want to get between my legs?"

He doesn't hesitate. "Yes. I don't care what you're wearing or how you smell. You're still gorgeous."

A small smile escapes my lips. "Well, I don't let them. Sex isn't on my radar. Survival takes everything I've got."

"So if you get by, why are you here now? And why'd you do

what you did two years ago?"

"Desperation," I admit. "We've got . . . a situation, and I need the money."

Andrew just looks at me for a couple seconds. His eyes are swimming with something I can't place. It looks like hurt and anger.

"Is this so you can fund someone else's drug habits? Or gambling?"

"No," I say indignantly. "Fuck you for assuming that."

"I'm just trying to figure you out, Quinn."

I glare at him, exasperated. "Do I seem like the sort to fund some deadbeat's habits?"

"You've got a dirty mouth when you're angry."

I shake my head silently. He looks at me for a few more seconds.

"I'm not taking advantage of a desperate woman," he says. "You look exhausted and worried. I want you to sleep in my guest room. In the morning, I'll make you breakfast and take you back to the hotel."

"And . . . that's it?"

"That's it."

A wave of guilt crashes over me. I took his money and definitely didn't give him what he expected.

"I'm sorry," I say softly. "It's not you."

"I'll take you to your room." He takes my nearly empty mug to the sink, sets it down, and then leads the way across his massive living room. We arrive at an open staircase, its steel steps held in place by thick, stationary cables.

Andrew ushers me down a short hallway to a room with a queen-size bed outfitted in white down. There are pillows for days and a vase of fresh pink tulips on the nightstand.

"Okay?" he asks. He's standing in the doorway, hands in his suit pockets.

"Yes. Thank you."

"There are pajamas in the dresser." His blue eyes are locked on me, his gaze intense. "Goodnight, Quinn."

"Goodnight."

He closes the door, and I hear his footsteps retreating down the hallway. My sigh isn't one of relief, but exhaustion. I didn't sleep well in the tunnels last night because Bean left after I told him and Bethy what I was doing tonight. He was so pissed he didn't come back until morning, and even then he wouldn't speak to me. And all day I've been tied in knots over what would happen tonight.

I throw the pillows to the floor and push the mattress off the box spring. Moving it across the dark wood floor leaves me breathless. I push it up against the closed door so no one can get in.

Forget pajamas. I haven't changed clothes for bed since I was sixteen. I curl up on the soft mattress and wrap my hand around the handle of my knife.

I think about Bethy. Has her fever improved? Is she sleeping? Is Bean being nice to her even though he's mad at me?

Questions swirl in my mind, and try as I might, I can't fall asleep. When I'm not thinking about my sister, I'm thinking about the tall, muscular man with dark blue eyes and short dark hair whose house I'm sleeping in. Is Andrew asleep right now? Was he disappointed in me?

It doesn't matter. Tomorrow morning, it's back to reality for me. And reality packs a cold, hard punch. I pull the down comforter over me, wishing I could bank some of this warmth for the nights ahead in the tunnels.

Chapter Five

Quinn

I'M SO WARM. It's light out and I need to wake up, but it's hard when I'm surrounded by such warmth and softness.

But wait—*why* am I so warm? It's winter. Panic slams into my chest, and I suck in a breath as I sit up. I'm in Andrew's guest room. My pounding heart slows slightly before I remember that Bethy is sick.

How could I sleep like that when my sister is sick? I was so worried about her, but somehow I fell asleep anyway. And slept like a rock.

I exhale deeply and run my hand over the smooth, cool bed sheet on the mattress. I used to sleep on sheets like this every night, before I ran.

"You'll pay for that, you little bitch. Run all you want. There's no escaping me."

But I've escaped so far, haven't I? Still, I want Bethy in my sight. Preferably within my reach. I can't relax fully unless I know she's safe.

I push the warm covers aside and move the mattress back onto the bed frame. I squint slightly, confused, as I look around the beautifully furnished room. The row of windows letting sunlight into the room is up so high that I can't see outside. Weird. I wonder what this old warehouse was built for.

There's an en suite bathroom, and it floods with white light as I flip on the wall switch. It's elegant but understated, with dark stone floors and light granite counters. I catch a glimpse of myself in the large mirror above the sink and grimace.

Dark eye makeup is smudged beneath my eyes, and my hair is going in several different directions. I open a tall cabinet beside the sink and find several brand new toothbrushes—still in boxes. There are also unopened boxes of toothpaste, new hairbrushes, razors, shaving cream, and bottles of shampoo and conditioner.

I think briefly about the women who've come before me, all standing here the morning after. But after a second, I move on, remembering my backpack is downstairs. I'll leave my shoes in here, grab my pack when I get downstairs, and then when I come back for my shoes, I can stuff the backpack with as many supplies as I can fit from the closet.

After opening a purple toothbrush and a new tube of toothpaste, I spend several minutes reveling in the minty bubbles as I scrub my teeth. Bethy and I always find a place to brush our teeth, but we ration toothpaste, so this is a nice luxury.

As I wipe the makeup from my face with a wet washcloth, I feel a fresh wave of guilt over not holding up my end of this bargain with Andrew. Should I offer some of the money back? The thought makes my heart hurt. We need that money so much. It'll buy Bethy a new coat and shoes, medicine if she needs it, and food for weeks . . . maybe even a couple months if I'm careful with it.

Maybe I'll offer him a BJ this morning. I'd rather do that than give back the money that's tucked safely away with Bean and Bethy at the hotel.

I finger-comb my hair the best I can and head out of the bedroom and down the open staircase. The smell of bacon in the air leads me into the kitchen, where Andrew is sitting at the table, wearing a gray T-shirt and reading something on a laptop.

"Morning," he says, picking up a mug of coffee and taking a drink. "There's bacon and eggs and coffee if you're hungry."

I fill the plate he left on the counter. There's so much food. I feel a stab of sadness that I'm about to eat this while Bethy and Bean are hungry. At least they have the money now, and maybe they'll even order room service before they leave the room.

Reminded of the deal we made, I clear my throat as I sit down at the table.

"So . . . I was thinking that we still have some time for . . . *you know*. If you want me to . . ."

He furrows his brow. Those dark reading glasses really work on him. His vibrant blue eyes stare back at me.

"No, what?"

I cock my head and arch my brows with impatience. "Suck your dick. Do you want me to suck your dick?"

His slight, smug smile tells me he just wanted to make me say it.

"That's okay."

"Do you not like me?" I ask defensively. "Is it because I'm a virgin?"

"I like you very much, and no, it's not." He glances at my plate. "Eat. I have something to discuss with you."

I bite into a piece of bacon, waiting.

"I've been thinking," he starts.

"You want the money back. And I get that, because I didn't—"

He stops me. "No. Just eat and let me talk, would you?"

My stomach unclenches. He said no. He doesn't want the money back.

"I have a proposal," he says, closing his computer screen. "I like you, Quinn. You intrigue me far more than most women do. And you could use a hand getting on your feet. I'd like to contract you to live with me for six months. I'll pay you ten thousand dollars a month."

My forkful of eggs falls from my hand, and the utensil clatters against the plate. He wants to pay me *how much*?

I clear my throat and pick up my fork. "I'm sorry, I'm not understanding. *Contract* me? For what?"

He gestures from himself to me. "For this. Like last night, but longer term."

"Oh. So . . . sex?"

The corners of his eyes crinkle as he smiles. "Hopefully. But I won't force you."

I rub my temples, overwhelmed and confused. "But . . . I was awful. We didn't do anything. Don't you want . . . you know, a pro?"

He shrugs. "Like I said, I like you. You're genuine. You don't kiss my ass. And you don't think I'm going to fall in love and marry you. You're a pragmatist, like me."

I exhale deeply. "I don't know."

"You don't know if you'd rather stay on the streets or live here?" His slightly offended tone rankles me.

"I'm responsible for someone."

"Who? Your sibling?"

I wrinkle my face in a glare. "None of your business."

"Whomever it is, I'd think that sort of money would help. I'll pay you up front for the first month."

Ten thousand dollars. That kind of cash could do more than provide a warm place for Bean and Bethy to sleep. I could do a better job of hiding her from the people looking for us. I could afford a safer place than the streets and tunnels. She could eat well. Maybe even take some classes to catch up on what she's missed in school.

But we'd be apart. The thought crushes me. Bethy's been by my side for more than four years. She's a part of me.

"I need to talk about it with . . . someone," I say.

"Give me your word it's not a man." Andrew's voice holds tension now. "I'm not doing this if the money goes to your boyfriend."

"Didn't we do this last night?" I fire back. "There's *no* man. I'm talking about the person I'm responsible for."

After a pause, he asks, "How long do you need to decide?"

"I don't know . . . Just today, I guess. Can I let you know in the morning?"

"Sure. Where can I meet you?"

"Um . . ."

"I'll put you up at a hotel for tonight."

"The one Dawson got me so I could get ready for last night?"

"Sure. We'll extend it for the night, and I'll meet you in the lobby in the morning. Nine AM."

His gaze holds such intensity I feel unnerved. It's so strange, being looked at this way. Not only as a person, but as a woman. Worthy of attention and caring. I've never felt it before.

I eat my breakfast, trying not to get ahead of myself. Bethy is very attached to me, and she might freak out over this idea. But the thought of taking care of her—really taking care of her—for the first time since we left home more than four years ago has me excited. She could be warm, fed, *safe*. No more sleeping with one eye open because I'm terrified someone will try to rape or murder my little sister.

It's not really possible to put a price on that.

Andrew

I'M BEING KIND of an asshole on the drive to the hotel. Instead of trying to put Quinn at ease and sell her on the idea of living with me, I'm just staring out the windshield in silence.

She's not sure? Living on the brutal streets of New York City is a close contest with living at my place and being paid well for it? I've been more than understanding with her. Hell, I jerked off alone in my bedroom last night when I'd been planning on a night of great sex with her.

Quinn's not like other women. I'm intrigued and more than a little attracted to this mysterious woman with a hunting knife strapped to her thigh.

"I thought rich guys had someone drive them places," she murmurs.

I clench the steering wheel of my Land Rover and glance over at her. "Would you like to see a bank statement to confirm my net worth?"

Her lips curve in the tiniest smile of amusement. "No, it was just an observation."

"I use a driving service to and from my office and anything in the city that requires parking. But I like driving, too."

"I would too, if I had a car like this."

I take a deep breath as I slow to a stop in traffic. "What can I say to persuade you? Whomever this person you're responsible for is, do you need to bring them along?"

She gives me a look of horror. "No. I just need some time to think about it."

I want to offer her more money. The hotel is less than a half mile away, and I don't want her getting out of this car without a deal in place. She could just leave the hotel before our meeting tomorrow, and I'd never see her again.

But, no. I shift in my seat, deciding I'm not offering more money. I've made her a great offer—one most women in her situation would jump at. If she doesn't take it, fine by me.

We make the rest of the trip in silence. I pull up in front of the hotel and wave off the valet who approaches. Quinn reaches for her door handle.

"I'll get that for you," I offer.

She opens it. "I've got it. I'll see you in the morning, Andrew."

"In the lobby? You'll be there?"

"Nine o'clock. I'll be there."

I pass her my business card, on which I've written my cell number.

She takes it and slides out of the car, meeting my eyes before closing the car door. I see curiosity swimming in those brownish gold eyes and a hint of a smile on her lips.

And then she's gone, slipping through the front door of the hotel. She went in with her head down, and no one even looked at her.

I stare at the door for a few seconds before pulling away from the curb. The farther I get from the hotel, the more out of control I feel.

And there's nothing I loathe like that feeling. Of all the things I've set my sights on, Quinn feels like the wild card. The one thing I may not be able to buy or charm. The challenge of it runs warm and fierce through my veins.

If she says no, it won't be fine by me at all.

Chapter Six

Quinn

"FUCK THIS SHIT."

Those are the first words out of Bean's mouth when I tell him about Andrew's proposal.

"Look," I say, "this is a chance—"

"A chance for you to become some rich guy's *slut*," he says bitterly.

I take a step closer to him. "Don't you ever say that word to me again. Not ever, Bean. We've both done things we're not proud of in the name of survival."

"Not that, though." There's a pleading note in his tone now. "One night was bad enough, but six months?"

Bethy is curled up on the bed, crying softly. I go to her, sitting down and wrapping my arms around her lithe body.

"It's okay," I say. "I haven't said yes or no yet. This is our chance to talk about it."

"I say *hell no*," Bean says. "This is some bullshit if you—"

I cut him off with a glance. "Give Bethy a chance to talk."

She sniffles and takes a few seconds to compose herself. "I don't want to eat food paid for by you having to sell yourself. I'd rather be hungry."

Bean nods approvingly.

"It's not like that, though, you guys. We didn't even do anything last night. He only wants sex if I want to do it."

"So do you want to? Do you like him?" Bethy asks.

"No." Bean answers for me. "She got too much integrity to like that sort of man."

He means well. I know he does. Bean has had our backs through times when it would have been much easier for him to dump us off and just take care of himself. And he tends to be a knee-jerk reaction kind of person.

"He seems pretty okay," I say, choosing my words carefully. "And if I don't like being there, I can just leave."

Bean scoffs angrily. "Yeah, this dude just gonna let his *investment* walk out the door?"

"I'll leave on my own terms if I have to."

Bethy sighs and meets my eyes. "I'd just miss you so much."

"Me too." I run a hand over her dark hair. "But it's only six months, and the money would last us until you're eighteen. When I'm done, I'll meet you guys in Mexico, and we can all start a new life."

My sister nods slightly. "That's where Bean and I would go from here?"

"Yes. That little town there he's always talking about. The one by the beach. We can write letters. I want you guys to write me through Anna, and I'll do the same."

"Why?" Bethy's voice quakes nervously.

"Just to be safe. I don't want anyone able to track your location. This way, if someone finds me, they won't be able to find you, too."

"You're doing this, aren't you?" Bean asks, a vein popping out on his forehead. "This is just some bullshit to make us feel like we all decided."

"What do you think I should do?" I shoot back at him. "Bethy needs a better life than this. We all do. I'm fucking tired of eating trash and being cold. Aren't you?"

He's quiet for a few seconds. "Yeah. But I'd rather us be cold and safe together."

"I'll be safe. I promise you. You know how good I am at taking care of myself, Bean. I just need to know you'll take care of Bethy."

He nods. "'Course I will. You two's all I got in this world."

The emotion in his voice tugs at my heart. "This is a job. An easy job I'm being paid extremely well for. It's the break we've been waiting for."

"Does Andrew know who you are?" Bethy asks me.

"No. And he won't."

"What if this guy wants you more than six months?" Bean asks.

"I'm done after six months," I say emphatically. "That'll be enough money to last us."

Silence settles around the small, poshly decorated hotel suite. It's broken by a deep, hacking cough from Bethy. I lock eyes with Bean as I rub a hand over her back.

"So we'll do it?" I ask when she finally stops coughing.

Bean nods but looks crestfallen, his shoulders sagging.

"I trust you," Bethy says. "Whatever you want me to do, I'll do it."

"Good girl." I bend down to kiss her forehead. "I love you more than anything."

"I love you, too. Promise you'll write to me all the time."

"All the time. And you'll write to me, too."

She smiles. "I will."

"Okay. So this will be our last day together for a while. I'm going to ask Andrew to send a doctor here to look at Bethy."

Bean looks away, his jaw set in a tense line.

"And then," I continue, "we can watch movies and order room service."

Bethy grins and stretches out on the bed. "Sounds like fun. I miss movies so much."

I stand and walk to the door, promising to return soon. After taking the elevator down to the lobby and getting a strange look when I ask the desk clerk to borrow a phone, I call Andrew. I'm standing right next to the front desk on a cordless phone, the clerk likely eavesdropping on my call. But better him than Bean.

"Hello?" he answers in a deep, crisp tone.

"Andrew, it's Quinn."

"Quinn." His voice softens. "Hi."

"Hi. I need a favor."

"Anything."

I smile at his response. A wealthy businessman is sort of at my beck and call. How is this my life?

"Can you send a doctor to the hotel room?" I lower my voice and cup my hand around the bottom of the phone and my mouth. "Someone who will just treat someone without asking questions."

"Is it you? Are you okay?"

"I'm fine. It's not me." I'm practically whispering now. "Can you just do it? Please?"

"Of course. I'll make a call right now."

"Thank you."

After a pause he says, "I'll see you in the morning."

"See you then."

I hang up and hand the phone back to the clerk. Relief floods me. Finally, a doctor will see Bethy.

On the elevator ride back up to the room, I briefly consider asking Andrew to help Bethy and Bean get to Mexico. But, no. I can't risk telling him about them. The stakes are too high.

I'll have to rely on Bean's experience with subverting laws and hiding.

But first, I'm going to spend the day at Bethy's side. We'll laugh and relax and overindulge the way sisters should. For the first time in more than four years, I can just be with her and not worry about anything.

THE NEXT MORNING, I hug my arms tightly around myself as I ride the elevator down to the hotel lobby. Nervousness hit as soon as I left the cocoon of warmth in the bed I'd been sharing with Bethy.

I'm still wearing the clothes Dawson brought for my night with Andrew. The only other clothes I have are the ones I was wearing when I arrived at the hotel that day to be made over. They're too dirty and ragged to even consider wearing.

Not only am I self-conscious about wearing the same clothes for the third day in a row, I'm concerned that Andrew won't like me with no makeup and my hair tied back in a simple ponytail. But there's no makeup artist and hair stylist this time, just me.

When I step off the elevator and onto the fancy marble floor of the lobby, I see him. Andrew is standing with his arms crossed, looking at a painting on the lobby wall.

He turns as I approach. Again, he's perfectly put together, wearing khakis and a blue dress shirt with a dark wool coat. I have to remind myself that I can hold my own with him. It doesn't matter how rich he is or how broke I am.

"Quinn," he says, his eyes lighting.

"Hi."

"Did the doctor I sent take care of things?"

"Yes, thank you."

The doctor was young and exceptionally kind. He looked

Bethy over thoroughly and wrote her a prescription for an antibiotic. When my panic registered over being unsure I could fill a prescription without ID, he left and came back with the medicine.

I'd hated to ask Andrew for that favor, knowing he'd likely find out from the doctor that I was with a teenage girl and a man. But Bethy's health was more important.

"How about breakfast?" Andrew asks. "There's a place near here."

I nod. We walk across the ornate lobby to the tall glass doors leading outside. A doorman nods and smiles at me as he pulls the handle open. It's not the look I'm used to from hotel doormen. Usually, they either look right through me or sneer.

Andrew waits for me to walk through the open doorway and then he follows. He joins me on the sidewalk and points to the left.

"There's a little café a few doors down," he says, rubbing a hand over the dark stubble on his face. I can see there's something on his mind.

He walks so fast I have to scramble to keep up with him. I push my hands into the pockets of the coat Dawson bought me. It's so warm. I traded my coat for food in the tunnels last winter, and it's really good to have one again.

The only table we can get at the café is right in front of the large window that looks out on the street, and Andrew can barely fit his big frame into the small chair.

"Are your knees touching the bottom of the table?" I ask, amused.

"I'm fine," he says impatiently. "Quinn, what's your answer?"

"My answer is probably. I need to go over a few things with you."

His shoulders sink a bit with relaxation. "Of course."

A waitress stops at our table. "Coffee?"

"Please," Andrew says, turning over both empty mugs on our table. She pours steaming coffee into both of them. He takes a sip of his and then rests his forearms on the table, looking at me expectantly.

I clear my throat. "Can you pay me in cash or a blank check?"

"Sure."

"Is there anything you're not telling me? I don't want surprises later."

A line of confusion appears between his brows. "No. It's just what I told you."

"No sex with other men? Or women? I'm not doing that."

He shakes his head. "Absolutely not."

"No whips or chains or tying me up," I say. "That's nonnegotiable."

"I'm not into hurting women."

"Good. I get to keep my knife. And I can leave at any time I want if it's not working out."

He nods. "Of course. But if we go to a social function, you'll have to leave the knife at home."

"What kinds of social functions?"

"Dinners, fundraisers, cocktail parties. I have to do a lot of that stuff."

I hate the thought of going anywhere without my knife, but he's right. I can't take it to those kinds of things. Begrudgingly, I nod. But then a new worry sets in.

"Look, I have to be low profile," I say. "I can't be in photos as your date or anything like that."

"Okay. There's not a whole lot of that, anyway. I'm pretty low profile myself."

Somehow I doubt this tall, polished bachelor is very good at *not* drawing attention.

"Hey," Andrew says. "I know you need time to trust me. But Quinn, my home is highly secure. You'll be safe."

The waitress returns, and we both order. He gets oatmeal and an omelet. I get pancakes. As soon as we're alone again, Andrew continues.

"Most of the security at my place is unseen. But trust me when I say it's one of the safest places in this entire city."

I don't mention that it's *him* I was concerned about being safe from. I know how to take care of myself on the streets.

"So . . . okay," I say. "I guess it's a yes."

He smiles at me, his dark blue eyes warm. "I'm glad. I'll be sending Dawson to pick you up here later this morning. He'll take you shopping and get you settled."

"Okay. Are you going to work?"

"Yes. I always work Saturdays."

"So you're only home on Sundays?"

"Pretty much, unless I'm traveling for work. I come home most weeknights, but I actually have a small bedroom off of my office at work so I can sleep there if I'm working on a project."

This is sounding better and better. I get to live at his place and will only have to sleep with him sometimes when he's there. I've decided I'm good with losing my virginity to him. I'm twenty-one. I probably would've given it up to some guy in high school if I hadn't run.

The waitress delivers our plates, and we eat in silence. I finish first, still not used to getting food so easily. When Andrew is done, he gets some cash from his wallet and leaves it on the table.

"Ready?" he asks, standing.

I take a deep breath. "Ready."

Chapter Seven

Quinn

I'M CRYING. I didn't think it would be this hard to leave Bethy. She clung to me when I left the room five minutes ago. It was her brave smile when she finally let go that did me in.

Dawson ignores my tearstained face when he stands up from a bench in the hotel lobby.

"Quinn," he says. "Good to see you again. You must've done well."

I shrug.

"We have a lot to do today," he says.

"It's not your day off either, then?"

He laughs. "Sunday is my only day off."

"Is Andrew demanding?"

He leads the way to a dark SUV parked in front of the hotel and opens the door for me. After he slides in next to me and the driver pulls away from the curb, he answers.

"That's a tough one. I suppose he is. He wants what he wants when he wants it, and he wants it done just right. But he pays his people exceptionally well."

Don't I know it. I'm officially one of his people since I accepted the blank check that was delivered to the hotel's front desk in an envelope addressed to me earlier. It was harder than I'd expected it would be to pass that check over to Bean.

I trust Bean, sure, but money has never been on the table. Survival is all we've ever considered. And now that I've given him ten thousand dollars, will he remain honorable? It would be so easy for him to disappear and leave my sister high and dry.

I'd whispered in her ear as we hugged that she should go to Anna if anything went wrong. I planned to check in with Anna every day to see if Bethy had contacted her.

"So," Dawson says. "We'll be getting you clothes, shoes, makeup and a mani/pedi today. I'm having your cell phone delivered to Andrew's office, and he'll bring it home for you."

"I don't need a cell phone."

"Yes, you do."

I shake my head. Guess I'll just take it and never use it.

"Next week we're going to the doctor and dentist."

"The dentist?" I balk at that one. "And the doctor? I'm perfectly healthy."

"You need to get on the birth control shot."

I look at the rearview mirror to see if that statement gets me a glance from the driver. Nothing.

"Oh," I say, my cheeks warming, "but . . ." I can't complete the sentence; it's too embarrassing. I hardly know the two men in earshot, and I don't want to discuss sex semantics with them.

"What?" Dawson prods.

"You know, I just figured we could use . . . I mean, *he* could use . . ."

"Ah. No. He wants it this way. I have his clean bill of health from the doctor to put your mind at rest. He just had a blood test a couple weeks ago."

Well, with *twelve* women before me . . . yeah, I could see

how he'd need to be tested regularly.

"Why am I talking about this with you instead of him?" I ask, my cheeks still burning. "It's kind of . . . intimate."

"I'm Andrew's right hand. I take care of all the details in his life he doesn't have time for."

I hum my dissatisfaction with that. "Like me?"

"Yes. Make no mistake, Quinn, this isn't love. And it never will be."

"I don't *want* him to love me. I just figured for what he's spending—"

"It's pocket change to a man like him. He can hire people for his every need. I'm one of them, and you're another."

I sit back in my seat, feeling rebuked.

"I hope that doesn't seem harsh," Dawson says. "I'm just looking out for you. If you feel like you're the next *Pretty Woman* . . . don't."

I scoff. "Trust me, I know what men are about. I'm here for six months and not a day longer."

The driver slows to a stop. I reach for my door handle, but Dawson stops me with a light touch to my arm.

"Let the driver get it."

I want to open my own door, but I decide to choose my battles. Dawson leads me into an upscale boutique, where he kisses the saleslady on both cheeks.

"Taryn, this is Quinn," he says. I offer a quick wave, hoping it's clear that I'm *not* kissing her cheeks.

"Beautiful," Taryn murmurs as she eyes me. Her dark red hair is swept into an elegant knot, and she's wearing a dark suit. "Let me show you to a room, and I'll bring in some things."

The dressing room has textured fabric on the walls. Taryn sets a bottle of water on a small shelf and smiles.

"Make yourself comfortable. Be right back."

Dawson leaves with her, and I take a sip of the water.

Within a couple minutes, Taryn is back with an armful of dresses. I watch through the open dressing room door as she hangs them on a rack and passes one in to me.

"Start there. I'll be back," she says.

I run my hands over the delicate beading on the neckline of the black dress. I can't help feeling like I shouldn't be here. I'm a filthy homeless person who should be getting yelled at for even touching this dress. Not to mention that I hate everything clothes like these stand for. Money. Prestige. Exclusivity. It's a world I never want to be part of again.

"Why don't I hear you changing?" Dawson asks impatiently from outside the dressing room door. "We have lots of shopping to do, so let's move quickly."

I give him a dirty look he can't see through the closed door, then slip off my shoes and clothes and put on the dress. There are no mirrors in here, so I don't even know how it looks. I open the door tentatively and stick my head out.

Dawson snaps his fingers. "Out."

I sigh and walk over to the walls of mirrors at the end of the dressing room.

"Perfect," Taryn says softly. "It looks like it was made for her."

"What size am I?" I ask her.

She gives me a puzzled look. "Two."

Wow. I was a size six when we ran. I miss the curves I'd just started to develop then, now long gone.

"Okay, next," Dawson says.

"I think this one looks good," I say, admiring the drape of the long skirt and the delicate beads along the high neckline.

"We're taking it," he says shortly. "But we need more. Try on the next one."

I sigh inwardly and head back into the dressing room. Dawson is no longer the nice guy he seemed like when I met him. He just wants to manage me like another one of Andrew's details.

It isn't him I'm worried about, though. What if Andrew is different, too, now that I'm bought and paid for?

Andrew

I PULL A device from the console of my Land Rover and type in a code. The garage door behind the warehouse opens, and I pull in. Just as I park and step out, my phone buzzes in my pocket. I pull it out and see it's my mother calling for the third time today. For the third time, I ignore it.

A security guard nods as I walk past his booth. "Evening, Mr. Wentworth," he says, pushing a button to speak over the intercom. I nod at him through the bulletproof glass.

The garage sits beneath ground level, so I take the elevator up to the main floor. As soon as I close the door into the house behind me, the deadbolt slides back into place.

I'm in the coat room. It's rather ludicrous to have a room devoted to coats in a home for one, but I figure I'll sell this place when I'm older, and this might be a nice feature for those who will want to entertain here.

My phone rings again. I pull it out and shake my head as I read the screen. I slide my finger across it.

"Hi, Mom."

"I knew you were there, darling. Why do you ignore me?"

"I was busy."

"Too busy for me?"

I walk into the kitchen and open my wide, stainless fridge, taking out a bottle of water. "How are you, Mom?"

"Oh, you know, just the usual. Let's have brunch tomorrow."

Tomorrow is my first full day with Quinn. "Sorry, I can't."

"Well, this is absurd. You never have time for me, Andrew. You do realize you're the only family I have?"

She's a master guilt-tripper. It's made me into a master guilt-trip dodger. "I'll be seeing you Wednesday night at the fundraiser."

"If we even get a moment to talk, you mean," she says.

"I'll make sure we do." I open the water and take a long drink. "Hey, I need to go, Mom. See you Wednesday?"

"All right. I love you."

"Love you, too."

I end the call and set my phone and the water on the kitchen island. Dawson texted me when he dropped Quinn off an hour ago, so I know she's here. But I don't see her in the living room or the guest room she slept in last night upstairs.

"Quinn?" I call as I walk back down the stairs.

"Hey," she says, coming down the hall toward the living room. There's a book in her hand. "I was in the library. It's incredible, by the way."

"It's my favorite room in the house."

"I hope it's okay that I went in and borrowed this." She clutches the book to her chest.

"Of course. Make yourself completely at home here. There are a few doors you can't open because of the security, and everything above the main floor is inaccessible. I created a code for you to use the front door."

"Do you lease out apartments on the upper floors? Are there other people in the building?"

I pause for a second before answering. "Not apartments, no. But there is a business up on the next floor. I promised them confidentiality, so I have to keep all aspects of my personal home separate. Even the parking garage beneath the building is divided. Everything is soundproof and the security works both ways, so you don't need to worry about anyone getting in here."

"Okay, good."

"I have a voice-activated security system throughout the house. I have it set to learn your voice over the next few days. If you ever need help, just say my dad's name—David Alan Wentworth. It has to be all three names. Say it loudly and clearly so the system picks up all the syllables, like this." I say my dad's name, and a couple seconds later, I show her the screen of my cell phone, which is buzzing with a new text. "That's the system alerting me that it's on." I type out a message to my security people to let them know I was testing it.

She seems to be taking it all in when I remember one more thing I need to tell her. "Also, please don't bring anyone into the warehouse. The facial recognition program would alert security before you even made it through the front door with them."

Her eyes widen. "Okay . . . sure. I don't know anyone to bring here, anyway." She meets my gaze and holds it. "Can I ask a question?"

"Sure."

"Why all the security?"

"It's just my thing," I say dismissively. "The first business I started was a security program I wrote the code for."

"Oh."

I look her over. She's wearing jeans, a lightweight red cotton shirt that makes the light pink shade of her cheeks stand out, and sleek, dark flats.

"You look nice," I say.

She rolls her eyes and smiles. "Thank Dawson. He chose the outfit and told me to put my hair in this ponytail."

"You'll find it's nice to be taken care of."

She shrugs her slight shoulders. "It's not like I know what looks good these days anyway."

"Did he mention we're going out for dinner tonight?"

"Yes. I assume I need to change clothes?"

"A little black dress would be perfect." I glance at my wrist-watch. "We're leaving in thirty minutes."

"I'll get ready," she says, breezing past me.

I'm not changing out of the khakis and dress shirt I wore to the office, so I go into my home office and pour a small glass of brandy. I need to decompress a bit before dinner. Quinn has a magnetic pull on me that's hard to ignore. I want that tough, sexy woman in my bed tonight. The thought of being her first has taken over my fantasies.

But it's way too early. I have to wait until she wants it just as much as I do, and it's going to take time. She's different from the other women I've been with. Hell, she's never even been kissed.

I'm swirling the last sip of brandy in my glass a few minutes later when she steps into the open doorway of my office.

"There you are," she says. "Are you ready?"

She's wearing a bright green dress that hugs her lithe body perfectly and shiny black heels. I can't help eye-fucking her for a few seconds.

"You look great," I say, rising from my leather office chair. "Did my assistant fail to buy you a black dress today?"

She looks up at me as I approach her, a smile threatening to show itself. "He bought me several."

My cock throbs with awareness. She deliberately wore the green, then. Her resistance to bending to my will is surprisingly sexy.

"You know, I don't know your last name," I say, close enough now to smell her sweet, delicately scented perfume.

"It's Jones."

"Is it now?" I'm staring at her pale pink lips, trying not to think dirty thoughts about them. I don't need a hard-on I can't do anything about for the next several hours.

"Yes."

"Well, let's go toast our new arrangement, Miss Jones." I offer her an arm, and she slips her small hand around it.

"You're leaving the knife behind, I hope?" I ask on the way to the door.

"Yes, but I have a small switchblade in my bag." She holds up a tiny black purse.

I arch my brows. "I don't think there'll be any street-fighting at the steakhouse I'm taking you to."

She doesn't acknowledge my comment. I help her into the dark coat she hung over the back of the couch, put on my own, and then take her out a back door of the warehouse, where my driver, Roy, waits for us in a black SUV. I open the door for her, and she slides in.

From the moment I get in the backseat next to her, I'm thinking about taking her hips and pulling her onto my lap. I want her straddling me so she can feel just how badly I want her. If she'd let her guard down, she'd find my hands and mouth can take her to places she's never been. Dirty, sexy, mind-blowing places.

She's clutching the purse in her lap.

"Are you hungry?" I ask.

"Yes, very."

"Where'd Dawson take you for lunch?"

"We didn't have time for lunch."

"You didn't have lunch?" My aggravation bleeds through in my tone.

"We had a lot of shopping to do."

"I don't care. None of that stuff is worth skipping lunch for."

It's important to me that Quinn eat. The poor woman is too thin, and she's been hungry for too long.

"Don't say anything to Dawson," she says. "Please. I should have told him I wanted lunch."

"His job is to care for you. That doesn't just mean buying clothes and shoes. I expect him to treat you the way he treats me."

She laughs. "You're his *boss*. I'm his boss's piece. It's different."

"My *piece*, huh?" I can't help but smile at how direct Quinn is.

"Well, I'm sure I will be soon. I mean . . . that's the idea, right?"

Not fucking soon enough. This conversation is giving me a boner, so I shift in my seat and adjust myself.

"We're going to a fundraiser Wednesday night," I say. "You'll be meeting my mother."

"Oh, God. What am I supposed to say to her?"

I wave dismissively. "Don't worry, I'll take care of her."

"No photos," she says in a serious tone.

"You mentioned that."

She holds my gaze, and I have to adjust myself again. "When you're at work, should I be doing something? Cleaning the house?"

"No. I have someone for that. Just relax. You like reading, right? I have more than a thousand books in my library. And there's a workout room if you like to exercise."

She nods. I can tell she'll need time to adjust. It has to be tough to transition from the streets to a life where all your needs are met by others.

We ride in silence as she stares out the window. I have to break the ice.

"I can ask Ty to go check on your sister again if you're worried about her," I offer. "The doctor I sent over."

Quinn turns to me with a sharp look. "I knew you'd use that as an opportunity to pry. Don't ever mention her again."

"Ty called to tell me how it went. Why did you tell me you

had a sibling if you wanted her to be a big secret?"

"I thought I'd never see you again when I said that."

I can't help a slight smirk. "And now? What exactly is it you're worried about?"

"I mean it, Andrew," she says coldly. "Don't go there."

"This is going great so far," I mutter.

We both resort to staring out the window. I wish I would've ordered dinner in because there's no way this night will end well.

Chapter Eight

Quinn

DINNER WAS UNCOMFORTABLE, to say the least. The restaurant was so expensive there weren't even any prices on the menu. I was thinking the whole time about how many people could have eaten a decent dinner on what Andrew was spending on just the two of us.

I suspect the sex part of our deal will be easier for me than the part where I pretend to feel like Cinderella being swept off to a ball. If you ask me, Cinderella put up with her stepmother's bullshit for way too long. She should have rescued herself well before that prince showed up.

As soon as we got back to the warehouse, I went to my bedroom to put away the mountains of clothes and shoes I'd gotten earlier.

On Sunday, Andrew was in his home office with the door closed when I woke up. He came out for a sandwich at lunch and barely even said hello, then spent the rest of the day in there.

It's Monday now, and I'm reading my fourth book since getting here. I heard Andrew leave around sunrise, and I got up, too. I spent much of the night tossing and turning because I'm worried about Bethy and Bean.

Is she still sick? Is the cash allowing them to travel without identification? Have they drawn suspicion?

I won't be able to stop worrying like this until I know they've safely crossed the border into Mexico. It's killing me that Bethy's safety is in someone's hands other than mine, even if it's Bean, whom I trust completely.

If they get caught, it will all be for nothing. All the cold nights, the hunger, the people I fucking *stabbed* to keep us safe, will be a waste. I won't have a life left here or anywhere else if Bethy gets sent back home.

A little after ten AM I'm trying to read a page in my book for the fifth time when the front door opens. I walk into the living room and see a biracial woman with a pretty smile and graying hair.

"Hi there," she says. "I'm Turner. Mr. Wentworth's chef and housekeeper."

"Oh, hi. I'm Quinn."

Finally, someone I can talk to. Part of the reason I'm worried sick is because I'm all alone in this huge place with nothing to do.

"Pleased to meet you, Quinn." She walks over to a pantry in the kitchen and opens the door, taking an apron from a hook and putting it on. "I'll be cleaning and cooking, so don't mind me."

"What can I help with?"

She chuckles lightly. "Thanks for offering, but I've got it."

"No, really. I'll do anything."

She meets my gaze across the vast space between the wide-open kitchen and living room. "Mr. Wentworth would not approve of that."

I sigh deeply. Being a kept woman kind of sucks so far.

"Sure," I say. "I think I'll head out for a bit."

Turner just nods and gets to work in the kitchen. I get my coat and hat and leave through the front door of the warehouse, keeping my head down to block the icy wind whipping at my face.

It feels good to be walking. Normal. Some of the people I pass on the streets ignore me, but others look over. Some even nod or smile. Apparently an expensive coat and boots make me worthy of their notice.

I put a few miles behind me and realize walking in brand-new leather boots with heels is uncomfortable. I kind of wish for my old, worn-out tennis shoes. But at least I'm not cold.

Finally, I arrive at my destination and feel a warm sense of calm. If I have a happy place, this is it. I go inside and breathe in the familiar scent of paperbacks. This library branch covers four floors, and I take the stairs up to the third one.

Anna is sitting off to the side at the front desk. I smile as I approach her, almost tearful with happiness. Her dark auburn curls are tucked away behind her ears, and I see the glint of the silver chain she keeps her glasses on so she doesn't lose them.

She looks up and her face lights with happiness. "Quinn, it's so good to see you."

When she comes around the desk to hug me, I close my eyes and let myself be comforted by her familiar powdery scent and ample, cushy bosom.

"I have a message for you," she says when she pulls away.

"You do?" My heart races with excitement. How could Bethy have sent me a letter through Anna so quickly?

"She called and said she's safe in the place where your father's favorite baseball team plays."

My shoulders drop as the tension slides away. She's safe. They've made it to Chicago. Relieved tears sting my eyes.

"Mind if I ask what's up?" Anna says. "I've never seen the two of you girls apart."

I sniffle and gather myself. "Yeah. We had a great opportunity come up."

"Well, if you're happy, I'm happy."

I've known Anna since shortly after we arrived in New York. This library became a haven for us. It was a place to get warm in the winter and cool in the summer, all while losing ourselves in the stories that lined the walls of shelves. Anna took to us and slipped us food from her lunch when we were here.

"I'm happy," I confirm. "I needed a way for Bethy to send me messages, and I would have asked you first, but—"

She puts a hand up to stop me. "You don't need to ask. I'm glad to help."

"Thank you."

"I set aside a couple books for you," she says, heading back around her desk. "Maybe it was wishful thinking. Like if I saved them, you'd come by and see me. And look, it worked."

She passes me two thick paperbacks.

"These couldn't come at a better time," I say. "Thanks, Anna."

Someone else comes up to the desk, and she greets them. I fade into the background, heading for my favorite reading chair in a secluded corner of the floor.

Did Anna even notice my haircut, makeup, and nice new clothes? If so, she showed no sign of it. I smile as I settle into the club chair I think of as mine. It's not surprising, really. Anna never saw me as a homeless woman. To her, I'm just Quinn. The world could use more Annas.

BY WEDNESDAY, I have a new routine. After Andrew eats breakfast and leaves for work, I make a sandwich and pack it in my backpack. Then I lace up my old shoes and walk to the library, where I spend several hours reading and hoping a letter from Bethy will come.

Andrew gets home from work around seven every evening, and we eat whatever Turner made for dinner that night while making polite, meaningless small talk. When he asks me what I did that day, I tell him I read, which is true.

I leave to head home from the library early Wednesday because it's a long walk to the warehouse, and I have to get myself ready for the fundraiser tonight. I'm dreading it, but I know I have to put on a brave face.

When I walk through the front door, Dawson is pacing the living room as a man and a woman sit silently on the couch.

Dawson looks relieved when he sees me.

"Andrew's on his way home," he says with a note of apology. "I didn't know where you were, and I had to let him know you were gone."

"Am I a prisoner?" I demand, setting my backpack down.

"Not that I'm aware of." He gestures to the man and woman, and they get up from the couch. "The hair stylist and makeup artist are going to set up in Andrew's bathroom because it's bigger than yours. Go ahead and get into your gown."

I'd like to tell him I'll get ready when I please, but he's right; I do need to get moving.

"Your gown is hanging in your bathroom," he says, his face buried in his phone.

I step into the marble bathroom inside my bedroom and see that he hung a pretty but conservative dark gray dress on the door and left black heels and black lingerie on the counter.

Fuck him. *No one* is choosing my underwear for me. I may not control much in my life right now, but I'm holding on to a few things. I go into the walk-in closet that houses my new clothes and choose nude lingerie, a sleeveless, dark wine-colored gown, a black wrap, and black strappy heels.

I change into the gown and shoes and study my reflection

in the mirror. I'm too thin, my collarbone showing prominently in this dress. I'll just have to leave the wrap on at the event. My cheeks are still pink from the cold outside.

There are butterflies in my stomach, and I kind of hate myself for it. I feel excited about wearing this beautiful gown and getting my hair and makeup done. I've never done anything like that.

Maybe there's a little Cinderella in me, after all, but only as far as the dress and shoes are concerned. I'm definitely not looking forward to an evening out with the closest thing in my life to Prince Charming. Andrew has been cold and distant since Saturday night.

I'm on my way to his first-floor bedroom to meet the makeup and hair people when his voice makes me stop halfway down the stairs.

"Well, where the hell *was* she?"

"She didn't say," Dawson answers.

"Who drove her?" Andrew demands.

"I don't know."

"Are you taking care of her at all? I told you to see to her needs."

There's a pause on Dawson's end of the conversation. He's like a different person with Andrew. When he speaks, there's none of the impatience he always shows for me.

"I've been busy with your dry cleaning, delivering those reports, and—"

Andrew cuts him off. "Don't give me your bullshit excuses. Can I rely on you or not?"

"Of course."

I try to walk loudly down the stairs, and I clear my throat as I walk into the living room.

"Quinn," Andrew says, looking startled. "Is everything okay?"

"Of course."

"That dress is *not* going to work," Dawson says with a roll of his eyes.

Andrew cuts him down with a look. "She looks perfect." He turns back to me. "Where were you today?"

"The library."

His eyes widen with surprise. "The library? But I have a private library here."

"Well, I like the public one," I say with a shrug. "Your books are mostly nonfiction."

"How did you get there? Did you take a cab? I have a driver you can use anytime."

"I walked."

His lips part with surprise. Dawson cringes.

"You walked?" Andrew booms. "In the dead of winter? Through the Meatpacking District?"

I have to hold back a laugh. "I've been in far worse places, you know. And I had my knife."

"You don't have to walk everywhere and carry that damn knife anymore," Andrew says. "If you need something, just say so."

"I don't."

He rubs a hand down his face, looking frustrated. "Let Roy drive you. Can you at least do that?"

"I like walking."

"Use the treadmill in my gym."

"It's not the same. I miss the sounds and smells of the city."

He wrinkles his face in confusion. "You like the smell of car exhaust?"

"I'm used to it."

"You need to get used to being provided for."

I meet his gaze defiantly. "Don't make yourself out like some benefactor. We both know why I'm here. The only one providing for me is *me*."

A tense silence hangs in the air. We're staring each other down, both refusing to look away. I see Dawson edge out of the room from the corner of my eye.

We're alone now, and Andrew walks toward me purposefully. My hand instinctively goes to my thigh, though there's nothing there but the soft sheen of the gown's fabric. I clutch it nervously.

"I'm not gonna hurt you," Andrew says, sounding offended by the very notion.

"I know." My tone is more confident than I feel.

It's not that I think he's going to attack me right here. I'm not afraid of that. I'm worried about my sister, and I'm starting to think Andrew's sorry about the deal we made. He was interested in me that first night, but now he's gone all the time, and he broods on the rare occasions he is here.

"Are you ready to go?" he asks gruffly.

I lower my brows skeptically. "No. Dawson brought people to do my hair and makeup."

"Go, then. I'll get changed."

He turns for his bedroom, and I follow him. When he walks through the door, he gives me a confused look over his shoulder.

"They're—" I point over his shoulder "—in your bathroom."

After a glance through the doorway of his bathroom, he scowls. "I'll just use another bathroom."

My heartbeat feels like a snare drum in my chest. I want to ask him if he still wants me here. It shouldn't matter to me—I already have his money for the first month—but it does.

It matters so much. I can't stop wondering if my time on the streets has made me into a cold, calculating shrew. Can a man like Andrew feel attracted to a woman who glares at him and reaches for her hunting knife every time he gets within five feet of her?

I don't care about the things most women my age do. I can't get past survival mode. It's on my mind from the time I wake up in the morning and look around frantically to make sure I'm safe until I fall asleep trying to remember how it felt to have Bethy warm and secure next to me.

And yet . . . I find myself caring just a little about what Andrew thinks of me. I wish he could see my strength and realize I'm not a vulnerable little thing in need of protection.

The makeup artist washes my face and puts rich-looking makeup on my skin while the hair stylist curls and pins my hair into a glamorous style. I watch them in the mirror and realize no matter what I'm wearing and how much luxury I'm surrounded by, I'll never match this reflection on the inside. I'm just a ruthless tunnel rat.

All that worry over whether I'd be able to stomach sex with Andrew . . . and the reality hurts on a whole new level. He doesn't even want me.

Chapter Nine

Andrew

I CAN'T LOOK away from her. Quinn's naturally beautiful. Her big eyes, high cheekbones, and radiant smile set her apart from other women, no matter what she's wearing.

But when she steps into the living room, I'm floored. That dress was *made* for her lithe body and smooth, fair skin. Her blond hair falls past her bare shoulders, and her face is made up like a model in a magazine spread. Her smoky eye makeup and red lips make me drink in a heavy breath and let it out slowly.

So. Fucking. Sexy. That's what I want to say, but I don't think she wants to hear it from me. Not after the argument we just had. And not after the way I've been avoiding her since she moved in.

"Ready?" I ask instead, looking at my watch.

She nods and walks over to me, her shoulders squared confidently. It's a contradiction to the look of absolute panic on her face.

"You okay?" I ask.

"Of course."

Our eyes stay locked for a few seconds, and I feel my body unconsciously responding to her closeness. My dick begins taking over all the free space in my tux pants, and my muscles tense.

Dawson approaches and breaks the spell between us, reaching for my tie and straightening it. I give him an aggravated glare because my tie was already perfect.

"Car's waiting," he says. He lowers his brows at Quinn disapprovingly. "Where's your clutch?"

"My . . . what?"

He sighs softly. "Your small purse. The black beaded one I set out for you."

"Oh. I don't need it. I don't have any stuff."

Dawson gives her a look of pity. "Cell phone, lipstick, tampons?"

A blush blooms on her cheeks. "The only person whose number I have is Andrew, and he's right here, so . . ." She clears her throat. "And I'm already wearing lipstick, and it's not that time of the month."

"Still," Dawson insists. "You'll need touch-ups."

"If she doesn't want to bring it, that's fine," I say, settling it.

Quinn arranges the black wrap she's carrying around her shoulders. Dawson goes over to her and gently pulls her hair out from under the wrap and settles it around her shoulders again. I wish it were me doing it instead of him.

She gives me an expectant look, and I reach for her hand. Hers is shaking slightly when she slides it into mine. I give her hand a small squeeze as I enclose it in mine.

Dawson follows us as we head for the back door of the warehouse. He's hovering, which always makes me crazy.

"We're good, thanks," I say over my shoulder.

He stops walking, and I tell him to have a good night. He mumbles a thank you.

"Don't be nervous," I say to Quinn in a low tone as we

reach the door.

"I'm not."

She is. I can see it all over her face and feel it in her sweating hand.

As I slide into my dark wool trench coat, I think about how cold it is. I froze my balls off walking to a meeting a block from my office at lunch today since walking was faster than driving with lunch-hour traffic.

"You have a coat?" I ask Quinn.

Her cheeks flush with embarrassment. "Yeah, in my room. I'll go get it."

"Just wear mine." I wrap it around her and set it on her shoulders before she can protest. "It's warmer anyway."

"What about you?"

"I'll be fine."

"Do I look okay? Will I look like everyone else there?"

I lower my brows, confused by her question. "You look more than okay, and definitely not."

She presses her lips together. "I want to blend in. I *need* to blend in."

"A woman like you doesn't blend in, Quinn."

Her expression falls with disappointment, and my confusion grows. What the hell did I say wrong?

She's swimming in my coat. I can't stop looking at her. Even with her sexy dress covered up, she looks incredible right now. I want to pull her close to me. Hell, I *could*. I could do a hell of a lot more than that if I wanted. It's why she's here, after all.

But with her, it's different. From that first night, I haven't been able to do anything she doesn't want me to. I've paid women for sex before, but when it came time for it to happen, they wanted me. I knew by the way they licked their lips and moaned when my mouth met theirs.

Not Quinn. She wants me to stay the fuck away from her.

It's clear from her posture and the constant look of worry on her face. She's worried I'm going to jump her for sex, so I stay away from home as much as I can. It grates on me, having a woman think I'd take anything she doesn't want to give me.

Roy drives us to the event in silence. He's been working for me a long time, and he knows his job is secure, unlike Dawson, who frets. Roy worked for my parents before my dad died, and he stayed with us and became my driver when I finished grad school and opened my office downtown. He knows I hate small talk. When we arrive at the event, he gives me a nod when I step out of the car after Quinn.

I take her hand and squeeze it again. This event is particularly glitzy, complete with a red carpet. A few people nearby turn to look at us, and Quinn clutches my hand.

"What is it that gives me away?" she asks in a soft tone.

"What do you mean?"

She looks up at me, her eyes brimming with emotion. "Why don't I blend in? How can you tell I'm homeless?"

I'm taken aback, but I keep my game face on. I lead her away from the crowd, stealing a small space next to the building where we can talk alone.

"That's *not* what I meant," I say firmly. "You don't blend in because you're so beautiful, Quinn. Stunning. And you aren't homeless anymore."

Her lips shift upward just slightly. "If you think that, then why don't you want me?"

"You think I don't want you?"

She shrugs. "I don't know. You seem mad all the time."

I have to laugh at that one. "No. I'm just a serious person. And it bothers me that you look so guarded all the time and wear that knife like I'm going to attack you or something."

"I hardly know you, Andrew."

"If I wanted to hurt you, don't you think I would have by

now?"

She sighs softly. "I suppose."

"Look," I say, "I'm usually good at reading people, but I can't figure you out. You look nervous when I'm anywhere nearby, but you're asking if I want you. Are you asking because you want me to want you, or not?"

She gives me a slight smile. "I'm mostly worried about something else, Andrew. It's not you."

"Your sister?"

The smile fades away. "You used that doctor to spy on me, didn't you?"

"You said you have a sibling, and he said he treated a teenage girl, so I assumed."

She looks away, a cloud of cold air forming in front of her face as she sighs. "Yes."

"Anything I can do?"

She shakes her head, staring at the line of dark SUVs and limos waiting to drop guests off at the event.

"We don't have to stay here if you're not up for it," I say.

Finally, she looks at me again. "No, this is good. I've been going out of my mind with boredom. This might get my mind off things."

"You've been bored?"

"Turner won't let me help with anything."

"What, housework?" I balk. "You want to do housework?"

"I want to do *something*. Anything. I'm not used to not having any purpose."

I nod, about to answer, when the click of approaching heels makes me turn.

"Andrew Wentworth, why are you lurking over here like a . . . *oh*."

It's my mother, and she's coming closer to get a better look at Quinn.

"I didn't realize you were bringing someone," she says crisply.

"Mom, this is Quinn Jones. Quinn, my mother, Gina Wentworth."

"Nice to meet you," Quinn says.

"Is she a model?" My mother turns to me now.

"No. We were just about to go in." I keep hold of Quinn's hand and start toward the door.

"Well, that's a fine way to treat your mother," my mom says in the indignant tone I know all too well.

"You were rude to Quinn."

"I certainly was not."

Quinn tenses beside me. I squeeze her hand to reassure her and face my mother.

"You didn't even acknowledge her," I say.

Mom arches her brows, still taking in Quinn with her sharp gaze. "Well, I was unprepared to meet her, wasn't I?"

I just sigh deeply, knowing anything I say will prompt an argument.

"Andrew," Mom says, "Dahlia Donelson is looking for you. I told her you two could sit together at dinner."

The Donelsons are friends of my mother's, and she's been trying to fix me up with their daughter, Dahlia, since we were in high school. And finally, I've got a good excuse for avoiding her.

"You misspoke," I say. "I'll be with Quinn all night."

Even in the dim of night, I see the flash of aggravation pass over my mom's face.

"Are you coming inside with us?" I ask her.

She says nothing and strides past us, her heels clicking against the pavement. A surge of anger rises in my chest. Quinn is nervous enough without my ice queen mother adding another layer.

I'm walking too fast, a bad habit of mine when I'm pissed.

Quinn is rushing to keep up with me, and I'm about to slow down when a photographer locks eyes with me and arches his brows in question.

"Quick photo, Mr. Wentworth?" he asks, lifting his camera.

I hear Quinn suck in a nervous breath beside me. Holding up a hand to the photographer, I let go of Quinn's hand and wrap my arm around her shoulders. With her tucked against my side, I get us safely inside.

"No photographers allowed in here," I say as she slips my huge coat off her shoulders. I take it and pass it over the coat check desk in the lobby of the upscale hotel.

"There you are!"

I tense at the sound of the high-pitched voice of Dahlia Donelson. She's talking to me. Every time I hear her voice, she's trying to sink her long, bright-red claws into me.

"Save me," I mutter under my breath to Quinn.

She's giving me a confused look when Dahlia appears, arms outstretched, grinning and glittering in a flashy red dress.

"Where have you *been*, Andrew?" Dahlia says in my ear.

Her hug is too long, and I feel every inch of her body rubbing against me like a fucking stripper on the job. As soon as she steps back to look at me, Quinn slides her arms around my waist.

"I've been keeping him pretty busy, if you know what I mean," she says. I have to look down to confirm the confident, sultry-sounding words came from her mouth.

"Is that right?" Dahlia's smile stays plastered in place, but like the rest of her, it's fake.

"I'm Andrew's girlfriend, Quinn." She holds out a hand to Dahlia, and they shake.

"Girlfriend?" Dahlia practically chokes on the word.

"I convinced him to come out tonight, but he wanted to stay home," Quinn says, staring up at me with stars in her eyes.

"I'm telling you, he'd keep me in bed around the clock if he could."

"Is that right?" Dahlia says again.

"Don't get me wrong. I'm not complaining." Quinn gives Dahlia a conspiratorial smile.

I'm hard. I should be more concerned about it than I am, considering we're in the lobby of a hotel with a lot of other people, but all I can think of in this moment is Quinn's warm, soft body pressed against me. Even her insinuation that we've slept together makes my balls ache with desire for her.

I can't help seizing the opportunity to slide my palm down to cup her ass. It's firm and slightly rounded. She inhales sharply, and I sink my fingertips in farther.

"*Andrew*," she says in a mock scolding tone, "you just can't ever get enough, can you?"

"Of you?" I make no effort to hide the open lust I'm feeling for her. "Never."

I lean down and kiss her forehead. Her skin is smooth. It's all I can do to make myself pull away instead of tipping her chin up for a real kiss.

"Well," Dahlia says, clearing her throat dramatically, "I'll leave you two alone."

She heads for the hotel's ballroom, and Quinn gives me a questioning look.

"How'd I do?" she whispers.

"Amazing. Thank you."

"You were good, too. I actually thought I felt . . . you know, *something* against my thigh when I side-hugged you."

I laugh and squeeze her ass again. "No pretense here, Quinn. You excite me."

"I do?"

People are walking around us, and I realize we only made it about twenty feet into the lobby before Dahlia found us.

"We should go in," I say. "Do I have to take my hand off your ass?"

"That's up to you, isn't it?"

A silent moment charged with sexual energy passes between us before I answer.

"No. It's always up to you."

Her lips curve up in a smile. "I think your mother will be scandalized if we walk in there like this."

"I thoroughly enjoy scandalizing my mother," I admit. "And I'm thoroughly enjoying your ass right now, too."

Her cheeks are pink. I want to walk back out the front doors of the hotel and take her home. I want to find out what her ass feels like without the fabric of her dress in my way. What I really want is to have her ass in my hands while she rides my cock. I want her tits in my face as I bury myself deep inside her.

If I could just get her to want sex, I know I could fuck away all her tension and worry. I'm not great at making women feel good with words, but with my cock, I can make them incoherent.

Quinn deserves to feel that good. She deserves to be able to let go of all her doubts and fears and let someone else take over. As long as that someone is me.

We're walking into the ballroom when a business associate of mine greets me and holds out his hand for a handshake. I'm forced to move my hand away from Quinn.

She's like a different person in here, offering everyone we talk to a warm hello and a gorgeous smile. People are looking at us, and I know what they're all wondering.

Who is she?

It's unusual for a woman as beautiful as Quinn to appear on the social scene as a complete unknown. Usually, someone knows a little something about everyone who appears at these fundraisers. They're for the wealthiest New Yorkers, who attend just for the prestige of it.

We're deep in conversation with a US Ambassador when my phone buzzes in my pocket for the third time in less than five minutes. I see a slight flash of nervousness in Quinn's eyes when I excuse myself to check my phone, so I murmur in her ear.

"Be right back," I promise, brushing my lips lightly past her earlobe.

Christ, I want her bad. The coconut scent of her hair lingers in my mind as I step outside into a vacant conference room to check my phone.

I sigh with frustration when I see who's been calling. An entrepreneur I'm buying a company from is getting cold feet ahead of signing our deal next week. I've already spoken to him about it several times in the past few days. But I don't want to lose this deal, so I have to call him back.

He answers the phone and launches into a monologue about how hard it's proving to sell the business he built from the ground up.

"Have you reconsidered, then?" I ask, staring down the long, dark table in the conference room.

"Well, not exactly . . . I'm just wondering if maybe we need to renegotiate."

I rub my temple and mentally count to three. I've never had the patience to count to ten when I'm pissed.

"The deal's drawn up," I say. "At this point, it's either yes or no."

He sighs deeply and goes back into the monologue. I consider setting my phone on the table and going back out to Quinn, but that fantasy is short-lived.

I'm aware of every passing minute. I told Quinn I'd be right back, and this call is taking forever. Since I'm mostly on the receiving end of the conversation, I walk to the ballroom where the fundraiser is being held and search for Quinn. Given how little she's told me about herself, I'm concerned about her ability to hold one-on-one conversation with anyone without me there as a buffer.

I finally find her, and my moment of excitement upon seeing her long, lean body is cut short when I see who she's talking to.

Hell. It's my mother.

Chapter Ten

Quinn

"WHAT DID ANDREW say your last name was?"

Gina Wentworth is staring at me like a detective conducting an interrogation.

"Jones." I sip my champagne and glance around the room. *Where the hell is Andrew?*

"And who are your parents?"

I meet her steely blue eyes and hold her gaze for a few silent seconds before answering.

"The Joneses."

Her laugh is humorless. "So you're self-made, then? What is it you do, exactly?"

I shrug. "I have to finish school before I can do much of anything."

It's true. I just don't plan to mention I need to pick back up with my sophomore year of high school.

"Ah." Her brows arch with interest. "My son is dating a college student? How interesting."

She says the word "interesting" like it's some sort of communicable disease.

"And where did the two of you meet?" she asks.

"Dawson introduced us."

"I see."

A passing waiter holds out a tray of food, and I reach out to take something but then pause.

"What are these?" I ask.

"Bacon-wrapped dates, ma'am."

"Wow." I give him my most interested look. "What sort of dates are they?"

"What . . . sort?"

"I mean, are they . . . *American* dates or imported ones?"

I'm desperate to shake Gina Wentworth's questions, even if it means looking like a jackass with a pronounced interest in dates.

"I think, um . . . local, maybe?" The young server's brow is furrowed. "I know the chef tries to source local ingredients as much as he can."

"Does he? What kinds of local food does he use?"

A strong arm slides around my waist.

"Hey." Andrew's deep voice sounds against my ear, making me shiver slightly. "Sorry about that."

I take a bacon-wrapped date and thank the server, who looks relieved as he turns away.

"So how are you, Mom?" Andrew asks. "Been busy with work?"

"Oh, you know me. *Always* busy with work."

She looks between the two of us as though she's trying to figure something out.

"It's rather embarrassing when my friends are asking who my son is here with, and I don't know a thing about her," she says lightly.

"Feeding the gossip mill has never been my thing, Mother," Andrew says. "It's never been yours, either."

She purses her lips and says nothing.

"You ready to go?" Andrew asks me. I nod, trying not to look too eager.

"Already?" his mother asks, sounding outraged. "What about dinner?"

"We stopped by, and I made my donation already."

"Well, at least I got to see you for a bit."

I can see her stab of guilt hitting home with Andrew.

"Why don't you come by for dinner soon?" he says to her.

"Is it still just *your* home?" Gina fires back.

"Excuse me?" Andrew's brusque tone makes me stiffen nervously.

"Dahlia said your *friend* made a comment about convincing you to leave home tonight." She speaks in a low tone but makes no effort to hide a sneer in my direction. "Does that mean she's living with you?"

Andrew takes a step closer to his mom, and she cranes her neck to look up at him.

"I rescind the dinner invitation," he says in a level tone. "And you wonder why I don't want you to be more involved in my life."

He takes my hand and leads me away. I can feel tension radiating from him, and his eyes have taken on the dark blue cast of an approaching storm.

Andrew sends Roy a text, picks up his coat and drapes it around my shoulders again, and we wait outside in silence for five minutes. As soon as the SUV pulls up to the curb, Andrew opens the door and offers me his hand so I can slide in.

After he gets in next to me, he says, "Home" to Roy and then quiet fills the air around us again.

"You okay?" I ask after a couple minutes.

He turns to me. "I'm fine. I'm sorry about my mother."

"It's not your fault."

"The way she treated you was inexcusable. And you were already nervous, I'm sure she could see that."

I laugh and pat his knee. "Did I look like a deer in the headlights all night?"

He smiles, and I like knowing I brought him out of his funk just a bit.

"Not at all. You did great. But my mother knows when she's been an intimidating . . ." He sighs. "I'm not going to say it. I'm just sorry she treated you that way."

"It's not a big deal. I think she and Dahlia were just . . . caught off guard by me."

Andrew arches his brows, still smiling. He takes my hand.

"That was fun," he admits. "Seeing the look on Dahlia's face . . ." He laughs, and the sparkle comes back to his eyes. "I can only imagine the look on my mother's face when Dahlia ran to give her the full report."

I give him a sly wink. His thumb slides up to my wrist, slowly stroking my skin.

"You hungry?" he asks.

"Yes. I was hoping that bacon-wrapped date wasn't my dinner."

"What about pizza? There's a great little pizza parlor not far from here."

"Sounds great."

Roy drops us off, and I can't help noticing the man sitting on the sidewalk not far from the door of the pizza parlor. He's wrapped in a ragged blanket, and his greasy black hair hangs in sections around his bearded face.

I have to stop. I've got nothing to give him, but I want him to know I see him.

"Quinn?" Andrew says softly from next to me. He's lingering in front of the door to the pizza place.

"You okay?" I ask the man on the sidewalk.

He shrugs and offers a wry smile. "Been better."

I sigh softly, trying not to think about the cost of the dress and shoes I'm wearing right now. I'd take these shoes off and give them to him if they'd help.

Suddenly, I remember the coat. It's not really mine to give, but . . .

"Do you want this?" I shrug it off and hear Andrew exhale through his nose next to me. Is he aggravated? This is probably an expensive coat.

I feel his hand on my lower back then, and I know without any words that he's not upset about it.

"I got a coat," the man says, lifting the blanket to show me his gray canvas work jacket. "But thanks."

I see movement from Andrew, and I turn to him. He took his wallet out of his pocket, and he's peeling a few twenties off a roll of cash. When he passes them to the man on the sidewalk, the man's eyes light up.

"Thanks, man."

"Sure."

Andrew opens the door to the pizza place, and one corner of his mouth lifts in a smile. I'm warm all over, and it's not because of his coat.

"Take care," I say to the man. He salutes me and wraps back up in the blanket.

Andrew and I draw stares when we walk into the small storefront with a black-and-white checkered floor and a strong smell of pepperoni. Everyone else is wearing jeans, so we stand out in our formalwear. We're at the end of a long line, so I'm betting the place has amazing pizza. Just a whiff of garlic makes my stomach growl.

"What sounds good?" Andrew asks, leaning in close to me.

The only answer coming to mind is the faint scent of his cologne and the feel of his firm upper arm against my shoulder.

I look up into his eyes, wishing I knew how to put into words how I'm feeling right now.

My hand slowly makes its way up to his cheek, and I tentatively reach out to cup it in my palm. His dark stubble feels smooth against my fingers.

He's so still as I brush my hand across his skin. But within a few seconds, I feel him moving closer. He wraps his hands around my waist and tilts his face down.

When I feel his warm lips near mine, my heart races with awareness. His lips are soft, and he tastes faintly of chocolate. I don't care that we're in the middle of a crowded pizza place; I slide my other hand up to the back of his neck, my fingertips brushing across his hairline.

I feel a soft groan from him as he moves one hand up to my back, pulling me closer. His tongue gently touches mine and *wow, I really like it*.

After just a few seconds, he breaks the kiss and I'm staring up at him, breathless. His hint of a smile is back. At the sound of a very loud throat clearing, we both turn. The man behind us in line is looking at us sternly over the top of his glasses, pointing at the huge gap in front of us in line.

We step forward. I have to press my lips together to keep from breaking out in a grin. Why was I worried about not liking *that*? Not only did I like it, I want more.

While waiting for our pepperoni and extra cheese pizza to be brought out, we sit down at a high table with two tall chairs. I fold Andrew's coat before putting it across the back of my chair so it won't touch the floor.

"So," he says, still smiling.

"So." I feel myself blushing. It's kind of funny, really. I always thought I was made of steel when it came to everything but Bethy. And here I am, acting goofy over a simple kiss.

"I have to go out of town in the morning," Andrew says.

That wasn't what I'd been expecting him to say.

"Oh." I sit up straight and pull myself together. "Okay."

"Yeah, that call I had to take at the event was a guy getting cold feet over selling his company. I'm going to Hong Kong to meet with him and sign the paperwork before he can change his mind."

I nod. "Sounds like a good plan."

"I wish I didn't have to go."

"How long will you be gone?"

"It'll be a quick trip. Probably three days."

"Okay."

"Let me have your hand," he says, holding his hand palm up to the middle of the table.

I put my hand out, and he takes it in his, brushing his thumb over my knuckles. "Will you please let Roy drive you where you want to go?"

I smile. "Andrew. I don't think you understand what a badass you've hired in me. I know I can take care of business because *I have.*"

"So when someone pulls a gun on you, how does your knife help with that?" he asks sharply.

"Can we please not do this? I was feeling so good."

He nods slightly. "I know, I'm sorry. But I'll worry about you while I'm gone."

I cover his large hand with my free one. "I took care of myself and someone else on the streets for four years. We spent time in the tunnels. It doesn't get any more dangerous than that. I can handle myself, okay?"

"The tunnels?"

"We used to sleep in abandoned subway tunnels in the winter. I'd probably be there right now if not for you."

His brows lower and he flinches slightly. "Damn, Quinn. I want you to be happy, but I also want you to be safe."

"I want to be a person with free will." I meet his eyes solemnly. "Not a possession."

"Of course. I'd never want you to feel like that."

Our pizza arrives, and he lets go of my hand. He puts the first greasy slice on a paper plate and passes it to me. I've barely tasted the first bite, and I'm groaning happily.

"It's so good," I say.

"We should eat this every night for a while," Andrew says, sliding out of his tux jacket and hanging it on the back of his chair. "Or maybe just you should. I'd start to look like the Pillsbury Doughboy after a couple weeks."

I can't help laughing. "I doubt that. You look like you exercise regularly."

"Yep, every morning at five thirty."

"At the warehouse?"

"Yeah. I've got the small gym on the main level and a bigger one upstairs."

We eat in silence for a minute before I say, "So your mom seems nice."

He rolls his eyes and laughs. "Yeah, don't get me started. I love her and I'd do anything for her, but . . . I don't know. She changed after my dad died. Instead of selling his company, she decided to take over as CEO. The board of directors thought she was crazy, but I think she just wanted a challenge to occupy her mind, you know?"

I nodded. "I admire that, actually."

"Yeah, it was a connection to my dad in her mind, I think. And she kicked ass. She's still running it, and she's grown it by around three hundred percent."

"Wow."

I think about Gina Wentworth as we eat. Andrew is her only child. He's probably everything to her. I feel myself softening toward her.

We finish the pizza, and Roy drives us back to the warehouse. Andrew holds my hand again on the way in. He walks me to the bottom of the staircase and gives me a longer kiss, his hands roaming more freely down to my ass this time. When he breaks the kiss, I find myself wanting more.

"Goodnight, Quinn," he says, the fire in his eyes a contrast to the level tone of his voice.

"Goodnight," I whisper.

I turn to walk upstairs, and he watches me. I go slowly and sway my hips just a little, hoping he'll follow me. He doesn't.

I definitely didn't see this coming. I'm the one thinking about sex and going to bed alone. I decide it was probably just the kiss as I brush my teeth and change into a T-shirt for bed.

But for the first night since moving in to the warehouse, I don't lock my door. I don't even close it.

Chapter Eleven

Quinn

THE WAREHOUSE IS quiet. It's felt eerily empty in here since Andrew left early Thursday morning. He was gone when I woke up that day. I still have a vivid memory of the way he looked the last time I saw him. He seemed so much softer that night at the pizza parlor, and I want to see that side of him again.

I'd gotten a few *how are you* texts from him, and I'd told him what little there was to say about my day-to-day life these days. He hadn't told me much in return, but I was still excited about him coming home today. If nothing else, I needed the company. Andrew's staff was quiet, focusing on their work and keeping things cordial but detached with me.

It's Saturday, and the only difference between today and a weekday for me is that the library will be busier today. But as long as I can find a corner to hide away in with a book, I won't even notice.

I put on dark jeans, a long-sleeve T-shirt, and the new tennis shoes I bought. Andrew gave me a debit card right after I moved in, and though I hadn't planned on using it, I treated myself to these shoes yesterday. They feel like I'm walking on clouds. I'd forgotten how great brand-new tennis shoes feel.

Once I've grabbed my coat, hat, and purse, I'm on my way out the front door of the warehouse. Every time I go in or out this door, I'm wondering where the security cameras are and who's monitoring them. If I have a fuzzy scarf around my neck and face, will the facial recognition thing trigger an alert and send guys in suits running at me with guns?

It sounds dramatic, but I always take off my scarf when coming in or out of the warehouse just to be safe. Life sure is funny. I've gone from being on guard all the time to being *guarded* all the time.

Thursday morning, I briefly considered asking Roy to drive me to the library. But the couple hours a day I spend walking to and from the library are important to me. I like being part of the city again. The biting cold outside doesn't even bother me; I actually love coming back to the warehouse and thawing out over a giant mug of hot chocolate. Having *a place* is still a luxury for me, and I enjoy it more when I leave it and get to return.

About a mile from the warehouse, I stop in front of the window of a little candy shop and look inside. I've thought about stopping here since my first time walking to the library from the warehouse, but memories of standing here with Bethy have made it too difficult.

We'd been in the city for about six months when she stopped walking one day in front of the narrow store's window and pressed her face against it.

"I could stand here and smell that caramel corn all day," she said to me with a wide grin. "Don't you love it?"

"Yes."

We were hungry, but all we could do was stand outside the store and smell the food inside. My guilt over taking my sister from a place where she never had to be hungry to the streets of New York City had set in.

I'd already started to question which of the evils was lesser: the one I'd taken her from or the one I'd brought her into.

And now that I can afford to buy the sweets inside the store, Bethy is gone. I don't even want to try them without her.

I resume my walk, still thinking of her. She's always on my mind. It's especially hard being alone most of the time when I still don't know if she made it out of the country safely.

My worry about her had brought on thoughts of our mom. Did she worry the same way about us? I hoped she knew we'd left and not been taken, because I didn't think anything could be worse than fearing your child had been abducted.

She had to know, because we'd taken a handful of our things with us in backpacks. But still, your two underage daughters running away was likely a scary prospect, too.

I imagine she wonders whether we're safe—but never why we left. That's something she knows very well and has to live with every day.

By the time I walk into the library, my feet are icy cold. I feel the chill of winter weather more acutely now that I have a warm place to sleep at night.

When I get up to Anna's floor, I scan the shelf of new paperback arrivals, running my fingertips over the spines. So many possibilities. Knowing I can never read them all is one of the things I love about reading. Books will always be there for me.

I pull out a thick historical romance, and I'm heading to my favorite chair with it when I see Anna approaching.

"Quinn," she says in her soft library voice, "it's good to see you."

"You too," I say, smiling as she embraces me.

"Saved this one for you," she says, winking as she passes me a hardback with a plastic jacket.

I look down at the book, titled *Macroeconomics and You.* Then I glance back up with a puzzled expression, but Anna has already turned to leave. She gives me a quick, over-the-shoulder smile and walks around a corner before I can ask her why she saved this boring nonfiction book for me.

When I flip open the cover to see if I'm missing something, my heart pounds wildly as I find a letter tucked between the cover and the first page.

It bears a Mexican postmark. My eyes fill with tears, and I practically run to my chair, sit down, and open the letter.

Dear Quinn,

We made it! It took forever, but we're here. You know the name of the town, but I sent this letter with a messenger to be postmarked somewhere else. Bean said it was a good idea.

It's beautiful here. The ocean is warm, and it's the prettiest shade of blue green I've ever seen. I love the way the sand feels on my bare feet. I wish you were here. I hate that I'm here and you're stuck in freezing NYC.

Tomorrow, Bean is going to start looking for a job. I asked him if we're close to the people from the cartel who cut off his hand and he said no. I hope that's true. We're staying at a motel that's kinda a pit, but at least it's warm! When Bean finds a job, he's going to find us a better place to stay.

I miss you so much. Bean has been really quiet since we left. I think he misses you, too.

I hope you're doing okay and Andrew is nice to live with. If there is any way you could call me when Bean and I have a place to stay, that would be great.

I'll write again soon. I'll probably write so much you'll be tired of my letters, but it's as close as I can get to talking to you for now.

Love,

Bethy

I blink, and tears spill from my eyes onto my cheeks. I'm filled with happiness. I read the letter again, and then a third time.

She's safe. They made it. Bean came through for me in a way I'll never be able to repay him.

I carefully fold the letter, return it to the envelope, and file it in the black bag Dawson picked out for me when we got all my new clothes. I take out the phone and see a text message on the screen from Andrew.

> *Andrew: Just landed. Have to stop by the office before I come home.*

I get up from my chair and return the paperback to its spot on the shelf. I head back downstairs, trying to remember the name of Andrew's company. I saw it on a letter in the kitchen last week.

AD Wentworth Ventures, Inc. That was it. As soon as I hit the sidewalk outside, I type the business name into my smartphone.

I'm only 2.3 miles away. The phone brings up directions, and I arch my brows, impressed. This thing would have been handy when I was living on the streets.

It's been a long time since I felt carefree. But right now, I'm so carefree I can't keep the smile from my face. I speed walk past people on the sidewalk, checking the phone for directions and watching it count down the distance as I get closer.

I jog the last half mile, breathless as I double-check the address on my phone against the one on the nondescript downtown building. It's a match, so I walk inside.

As soon as I see the warm hardwood floor, I know I'm in the right place. Andrew had the same floor put in the warehouse. The walls are a rich, cream color with a few beautiful paintings framed in simple, dark wood frames. Even the light fixtures have a modern but sophisticated feel, all steel with exposed, clear lightbulbs.

"May I help you?" a woman asks from behind a sleek, modern desk.

She's beautiful. With her dark hair swept back into a knot and her charcoal business suit that looks like it was made for her, she fits right into this elegant place.

I immediately regret my impulse decision to come here. Andrew is probably busy catching up on work he missed, even though it's Saturday. He always works Saturdays.

"Uh . . . sorry," I say to the woman, my cheeks warm with embarrassment. "I think I'm in the wrong place."

"Jana," a deep male voice calls, "can you send me the paperwork on the close of the Wembley sale?"

It's Andrew, who has just walked around the corner. He follows Jana's gaze to me.

"Quinn?"

I smile awkwardly, wishing I would have dashed out the door when I had a chance. "Hi."

"Hey." He sets the folder in his hand on Jana's desk and walks over to me.

"I'm sorry," I blurt out. "I should have waited to see you later."

A corner of his lips quirks up in a smile. "No, I . . . it's good to see you."

"Yeah?"

"Yeah." He takes my hand. "Come back to my office."

Jana is eyeing me with open curiosity as we walk past her desk. Andrew leads me down a hallway, and I glance over at another beautiful painting, this one of a giant oak tree in a field.

He steps aside when we reach an open door, and I walk into his office. It has a massive, dark wood desk with neat stacks of papers and an open laptop. The walls are the same cream as the lobby, but the frames on them hold diplomas from MIT and NYU. Seeing them makes me remember my own dream of attending NYU. Instead, I'm a high school dropout.

"This place is more low-key than I was expecting," I say, turning to look at him. "I like it."

His eyes light with amusement. "What were you expecting?"

"I guess . . . a high-rise building with windows everywhere and sweeping views of the city."

Andrew just shakes his head. "Not me."

I run my fingertips over a dark wood bookcase and scan the titles on the books. Many are about 9/11. Others are nonfiction business books. Aside from the diplomas, there doesn't seem to be a personal touch to this office.

"You want me to hang up your coat?" he asks.

I nod, slide it off, and hand it to him. He hangs in on an antique-looking wooden coat rack in a corner and walks back to me.

"I think I surprised your, uh . . . Jana."

"Yeah, we don't get much walk-in traffic." He gestures to a leather wingback chair, inviting me to sit down, but I shake my head no. "She's my receptionist. I have a couple other people on staff, but they don't work Saturdays."

"How was your trip?" I ask, suddenly feeling nervous.

"Good. A lot of time in the air, but I was able to work on the plane."

He crosses his arms, and I hate how awkward it feels between us. I wanted the newfound warmth from our night together and the kisses we shared to stay with us.

"So I came because I got some good news," I say, taking a deep breath, "and I just wanted to see you."

"Good news?"

I nod but don't elaborate.

"I see," he says softly. "Well, that's great. It's really good to see you, Quinn. I missed you."

The tenderness in his tone makes me jump forward and throw my arms around him. "I missed you, too."

He laughs and wraps his arms around my back. We hold on to each other for a full minute, his nose brushing over my hair and my hands running up and down his back.

This feels good. It's been so long since I've felt the sense of security I have with Andrew. Despite the paid nature of our relationship, I know if I needed something, he'd be there in an instant. Part of me wishes I could take a chance and trust him with my past, but I can't. There's too much at stake.

I pull away from him, leaving my palms on his chest. My gaze roams around the room, and I come to a conclusion that makes me furrow my brow.

"There are no windows here."

Andrew shrugs. "Not much of a view. Just an alley."

"The warehouse is the same way. All the windows are high up."

"I'm a very private person, Quinn."

Having no windows seems hyperprivate, but I just smile. I'm finding that Andrew is a hard man to know. I can respect that since I'm the same way. But given that we're coming up on the end of the first month of six together, I'd like to try. I'd like to find a way to soothe the deep loneliness I feel for Bethy and Bean.

"Is Roy outside?" Andrew asks. His hands rest loosely on my hips, and I like the way it feels.

"Um . . ."

"I know he's not. I've checked in with him every day, and he says you haven't ridden with him even once."

I sigh deeply. "I know. I know you want me to, but like I

said, walking is important to me. I'm used to walking miles every day. I need the freedom it gives me from being indoors all the time."

He nods, his lips set in a reluctant line.

"I bought new shoes," I say, stepping back and looking down at them. "With the card you gave me."

That gets me a small smile.

"Those are nice. I'm glad you went shopping."

"They were on sale."

He rolls his eyes. "Quinn, buy anything you want. I'm quite wealthy, okay?"

"I know, but . . . that's not me anymore."

"Anymore?"

I look around the room, trying to find something I can use for a subject change. After a few seconds, Andrew asks, "Have you had lunch?"

"No."

"Why don't I call Roy, and we'll go get something to eat? I'm about done with work anyway."

"That sounds good."

While he's calling Roy, my phone buzzes and I check the screen. There are a couple text messages waiting there.

Dawson: Why haven't you responded to my texts?

Dawson: Quinn . . . I need to make salon and gown-fitting appointments for you. Text me back.

I tuck the phone back into my purse. Dawson's been hounding me since Andrew left, wanting to get me waxed and dyed and fitted into a glamorous woman for Andrew's return. I've grown tired of him treating me like a doll he can fix up as he pleases, so I've been ignoring him.

"What's with the frown?" Andrew asks. "Everything okay?"

"Everything's great."

It really is. Bethy is safe in Mexico, and Andrew is back. Everything in my small world feels right.

Chapter Twelve

Andrew

QUINN IS DIFFERENT now. She's lighter. The good news she got has obviously taken a weight from her shoulders. I can only assume it was about her sister.

Over soup and sandwiches at a deli near my office, she's smiling more than I've ever seen her smile. She's even poking fun at me and laughing. I like this side of her.

"So Hong Kong . . ." She takes a sip of her hot tea and studies me. "Did you have to take someone to translate for you?"

"No. Most of the people I met with speak English. There's one guy who prefers Cantonese, and I'm passable with it."

She arches her brows, looking impressed. "Cantonese? Really?"

"Just enough to get by."

That's not actually true. I'm fluent, but I don't want to sound like I'm trying to impress her. If she is impressed by me, I don't want it to be about my work or my money.

"Have you ever been to China?" I ask her.

She laughs lightly. "No. My family took some vacations to a resort in Mexico when I was little. I've never left the country other than that."

I watch her expression to see if it turns remorseful. She's been so vigilant about not sharing her personal life with me. But she seems so at ease right now, without a hint of regret.

"You're welcome to join me next time," I say. The thought having her alone in the back of a Lear for all those hours in the air is *very* appealing.

Another laugh from her. "You mean go to China? Me?"

"Sure. We could go sightseeing if you'd like."

Her smile fades. "Thanks for the invite. It's a really nice thought. I couldn't, though."

"Of course, you could."

"Actually . . . I *couldn't*. I don't have a passport."

"That's an easy fix."

She shifts her gaze away from mine. "Not in my case."

"Should we skip the part where I ask why and you tell me you don't want to talk about it?" I ask lightly.

"Yeah, let's skip that."

"If you could go anywhere in the world, where would you want to go?" I ask, watching as she raises her mug of tea up to take a slow sip. She likes hot tea so much she ordered it rather than dessert at the end of our lunch. And she always drinks it the same way, with both hands wrapped around the mug.

"Hmm . . ." She lowers the mug, and her lips curve up in a smile. "Anywhere in the world? Maybe New Zealand. Or Antarctica."

"Antarctica?" I give her a confused shake of my head.

"Yeah. Maybe. Or Iceland."

"So you'd like to go far away," I surmise. "You like to feel hidden."

Her expression turns serious. "I guess that's true."

"What are you hiding from, Quinn?"

She shrugs. "We're all hiding from something, don't you

think? Some people don't even know they're doing it."

I think about her words. She's pretty philosophical for a twenty-one-year-old. The other women I've dated now seem flippant and vacant compared to her.

"I'm not hiding from anything," I say. "I wake up every morning planning to take life by the balls and squeeze."

"That sounds unpleasant," she says with a laugh.

"Nah. Long as it's not *my* balls."

"Well, ball squeezing aside, I think you have fears just like the rest of us."

"Yeah? What is it you think I'm afraid of?"

I wait, eager to see what she'll come up with. Very few people know me at all. Only a small handful *really* know how fearless I am when it comes to accomplishing my goals. Quinn isn't one of them.

"Intimacy." She says it with finality, like there's no debating that it's true.

I sit back in my seat. "Intimacy?" I look from side to side and then lower my voice. "You mean *sex*? Baby, I can assure you it's not *my* fear standing in our way. I'm ready to go. Right now."

"Not sex. Anyone can do that. I'm talking about emotional intimacy."

I fight the urge to roll my eyes. "Yeah, that's not my thing. Not because I'm afraid of it, though."

"Okay."

She doesn't believe me, I can tell by her tone. It annoys the hell out of me.

"As for the sex," she says softly, "I'm not afraid. Just so you know."

"No?" My annoyance melts away. "What's, uh . . . holding us back, then?"

"Now that you're back . . . nothing. I've been thinking about you since that night."

"When I kissed you?"

"Yes."

I shift my hips, my dick needing more space all of a sudden.

"I've been thinking about it, too," I say. "A lot."

The air is thick between us, laced with wanting that, for me, borders on need. It's been more than a month since I've had sex, and I've spent almost four weeks wanting Quinn every time I look at her.

"So . . ." Her voice is nearly a whisper. "Maybe we should . . ."

"Go shopping in Tribeca?" I say, against my every instinct. "There's an art gallery there I'd like to take you to. And a furniture store."

"Oh. Okay."

"What else would you like to do?" I ask, leaning to the side so I can take my wallet from my pants pocket. "Carriage ride?"

She shakes her head. "I hate the way those poor horses are treated."

"Oh. Right. Well, you pick something then. Anything. Broadway show?"

Her eyes light with happiness. "Can we go to the movies? I used to love going to the movies."

"We can definitely go to the movies."

At the furniture store, Quinn runs her fingertips over the smooth lines of the industrial-style steel and wood furniture. She helps me try out chairs until we settle on a perfect one for the library. It's a chaise the furniture maker will upholster in the dark chocolate shade of leather Quinn chose.

"That's your favorite?" I ask her with a skeptical glance.

She shrugs. "It looks like the other furniture at the warehouse. You want it to fit in, don't you?"

"Fitting in is overrated. What's your favorite color?"

"Purple," she says, arching her brows in challenge.

"Purple," I say to the store owner.

"Certainly." He flips through several leather swatches and lands on one. "I have this nice eggplant shade."

"You like?" I ask Quinn.

"I do."

"We'll take it," I say, handing the man a business card. "You can arrange for payment and delivery with my assistant, Dawson."

I take Quinn's hand, and we walk the half mile to the art gallery I've been to a few shows at. Tiny snowflakes are flying outside, and a few of them sparkle in her blond hair as we walk through the big double doors of the gallery.

"Mr. Wentworth," the curator says, giving me a polished smile. "So nice to see you again."

Her bright red hair is secured in a knot at the nape of her neck, and she wears a dark green suit. I can see dollar signs written all over her face, though she's trying to look casual.

"Hi," I say, following Quinn to a display of gritty black-and-white portraits.

"Anything I can help with?" the curator asks. "I'm Meg, by the way."

"Just browsing."

She nods and returns her attention to the clipboard she's holding.

"Wow," Quinn says softly.

I follow her gaze to a portrait of an old woman with deep lines in her weather-worn skin. Her dark eyes stare not just straight at the camera, but through it. They tell a story of resilience. An open field with freshly sown rows is the photo's backdrop. Her age-spotted hand is wrapped around a primitive-looking farm tool.

A glance at an engraved silver sign enlightens me about this series of portraits.

"All taken at a small village in Guatemala," I murmur. "They're fantastic."

Quinn is still looking at the woman, seemingly entranced by her. And I'm entranced by the emotion swimming in Quinn's hazel eyes.

"I'll buy it for you," I offer.

She gives me a sideways smile and then shakes her head. "No, but thanks."

"You sure? I can tell you love it."

She sighs softly. "I just feel like I know her."

Meg is hanging at just the right distance to casually eavesdrop.

"Beautiful, aren't they?" she says with a practiced smile.

I nod and lay a hand on Quinn's slight shoulder. "Do you just like this one, or all of them?"

She looks up at me with a serious expression. "I don't want you to buy it, okay? It should be here for everyone to see."

"This entire exhibit *will* sell," Meg says a little sharply. "It's only a matter of who will be the winning buyer."

Quinn narrows her eyes slightly.

"Well, it won't be us," I say, sliding my hand back into hers.

She squeezes my hand, and I lead the way out of the gallery.

"I hate her," Quinn mutters as we step onto the sidewalk. "I think she and Dahlia should hang out."

I laugh and take out my cell phone to text Roy. "There's an idea."

"They could form a Bitches Anonymous group."

I type out the address of a nearby corner for Roy to pick us up at and then turn to Quinn.

"You dislike . . . what was her name again?"

"Meg."

"Right, *Meg* . . . that much just from that one encounter?"

"Not everything should be for sale. It's disgusting, really.

That woman struggles just to exist, and some rich person will pay more money for that picture than she can ever imagine having, and they'll hang it up in their house as a decoration."

I think about her words for a few seconds, realizing she's right, but I never would have seen it that way without her pointing it out.

"Is that what you think of me?" I ask, feeling a sick churning in my gut. "Do you think I'm profiting from your misery?"

She turns to me with wide eyes. "Not at all. No, it's not remotely the same. You're respecting me and taking care of me and . . . *paying* me. That woman will get nothing for that photo."

"Maybe it'll help create awareness of the need for assistance in Guatemala."

Quinn arches her brows skeptically. "I doubt that. Most people ignore the needy."

"Did you feel ignored when you were homeless?"

"I didn't just *feel* ignored, I *was* ignored." A couple beats of silence pass and she says, "What do you do when you pass a homeless person on the street?"

I meet her eyes for just a second and then look away, feeling sheepish. She's right. Truth be told, I ignore just about everyone when I'm walking down the street, but it's not right to brush past every person I see who could use a hand. I can't help all of them, but that doesn't mean I can't help some of them.

Roy pulls up, and we slide into the car and out of the cold.

"Head to the nearest movie theater," I tell Roy.

He takes us to one with neon signs and windows that stretch up to the second story to show the escalators taking people upstairs. When we get inside, I tell Quinn to choose a movie, and she picks a big-budget action film. We pick up some popcorn and soda and step onto the escalator.

"I always wondered what it was like in here," she says, looking around at the ornate ceiling and moldings in the renovated old building.

"Beautiful reno work," I say.

She smiles at me. "I like that you love old buildings. Other people would tear them down, but you see their beauty."

"They don't build 'em like they used to. I just bought a spectacular building in Manhattan that was a dance hall during the Prohibition era."

"What will you do with it?"

I shrug. "Haven't decided. I just couldn't stand to see it made into a fast-food joint."

I like the look on Quinn's face right now. If I'm not mistaken, it's admiration. My money seems to mean very little to her. She's all about what I do with it.

The theater's not that crowded, so our seats in the top row are secluded. The movie's not bad, but what I enjoy the most is Quinn. Her small gasps during the exciting parts are cute as hell.

Roy's waiting when the movie lets out, and he meets my gaze in the rearview mirror after we get into the car.

"Home?" I ask Quinn.

She nods.

"Home," I say to Roy.

Quinn takes my hand and squeezes it.

"This was fun," she says.

"I thought so, too."

I slide my hand out from under hers and onto her thigh. The corners of her lips tilt up in a smile, but she doesn't look at me. I move my hand higher, my fingertips grazing her inner thigh.

Too bad she has jeans on. I'm dying to know what her skin feels like. Having her right next to me for all these hours has me wanting more. More than this, and more than I've had with her before.

Roy pulls into the warehouse garage, and I lead Quinn to

the elevator, pressing my thumb to the pad by the door. The door slides open, and as soon as we step on, I can tell by the look in her eyes that she wants more, too.

I want to back her against the wall of the elevator and kiss her, but I don't. Instead, I just let my gaze wander up and down her body, enjoying every inch of her. She slides out of her coat, her eyes on mine.

She's watching me watch her, and it's so damn sexy. I'm rock hard. It's taking all my self-control not to rip off her clothes and fuck her hard and fast.

"Make me a drink?" she asks as we step off the elevator.

She looks over her shoulder at me, and I tear my gaze away from her ass. "Of course. What would you like?"

"Whatever you think I might like," she says with a shrug. "I've never had alcohol before."

A pang of realization hits. Quinn isn't an average twenty-one-year-old woman. Her life experience is far greater than most, but she missed out on the coming-of-age stuff.

Part of me feels a stab of guilt for initiating her. But I'll take good care of her. Better me than some horny teenage boy who wants to get her drunk and take advantage of her.

I take out a small glass tumbler and mix up a screwdriver for her. I pass it to her, and she takes a sip as I take out a bottle of bourbon and a glass for myself.

"Mmm, it's good," she says.

When I look over, she's got the glass tipped back. As she lowers it, I see it's halfway gone already.

"Whoa," I say with a smile. "Slow down, champ."

"It tastes like juice."

"But it's not just juice."

Her cheeks pink a little. I take off my coat, toss it over a chair at the breakfast bar, and take a sip of my bourbon.

Quinn is standing in front of me, looking expectant and

hesitant at the same time. I set my tumbler down and cover the few steps separating us.

When I put my hands on her hips, her lips part slightly. I lean down and give her a soft kiss, sliding my hands around to her ass and cupping it like I've been wanting to all damn night.

She moans and slides her palms up my chest to my neck, over my cheeks, and into my hair.

My body is throbbing all over with the deepest desire I've ever felt. She's been hurt and left to fend for herself in a cruel world. And not only did she do that, she took care of her sister. She's been strong for so long, and now I want to be the strong one for her. I don't know how I got lucky enough to be here with her right now, but I'm overwhelmed with gratitude.

I pull away and look down at her. "Can we go into my bedroom?"

She licks her lips and nods. I take her hand and lead her, practically breaking into a run. I can hear her laughing behind me as she jogs to keep up. When I turn around, wrap my hands around her waist, and toss her over my shoulder, she laughs even louder.

"Andrew! What are you doing?"

I run the last twenty feet down the hallway to my bedroom and lightly toss her onto my king-size bed. Her cheeks are flushed and her eyes are sparkling. I kick off my shoes, and she does the same.

I'm about to climb onto the bed when I notice her ear-to-ear smile shrinking. A crease forms between her brows.

"Is that . . . ?"

She's staring at my crotch, where my erection is prominently outlined against my khakis.

"Yeah," I say with a grin. "You really bring him to life."

"Jesus. You're going to kill me with that thing."

She looks genuinely horrified.

"I promise I won't. No sex tonight, anyway."

"No sex?" The crease gets deeper. "But I thought . . . ?"

I lie down on the bed and grab her hips, pulling her light body onto mine. The feel of her against my cock makes me groan.

"Stop thinking," I say, pulling down on her hips as she straddles me. Her lips part again, and her eyelids close.

"That feels good," she murmurs.

"Just feel. Tonight, just feel."

She lets her head fall back and grinds her hips against me. It's hot as fuck seeing her on top of me like this. I slide my hand under her shirt, my fingertips grazing across her lean, smooth stomach. She sighs softly.

Much as I want to let her do all the driving, I can't help my controlling nature. I sit up and push her shirt all the way up and then off over her head. When I resume my grip on her hips, she moans loudly and grinds against me again.

I kiss her breasts through the satin fabric of her bra, my tongue tracing the seams of the fabric and circling her nipples.

The sounds of heavy breathing and moaning fill the room. I unclasp Quinn's bra, slide it off, and toss it to the floor, taking one of her tight, pink nipples between my lips and sucking on it.

"Oh, God," she says with a moan. "Andrew . . ."

She grabs my cheeks and kisses me with a fervor I've never seen in her. Her tongue seeks mine, and her hips continue the sweet, torturous grinding that keeps my cock and balls aching for more.

I slide a hand down the back of her jeans and grip her ass. She moans into my mouth and then presses her palms to my shoulders and pushes me down to the bed.

Me. Pushed down to the bed by a woman. It's never happened. I'm the one who issues the orders in bed, not the one who takes them. But what Quinn wants from me, she'll get.

She bites her lower lip for just a second. I'm reaching for her small but absolutely perfect breasts when she shakes her head, smiles, and slides off of me.

My groan of frustration morphs into something else as she unfastens my pants. She pulls them off, boxer briefs and all, and I frantically unbutton the dress shirt I'm wearing and work my way out of it.

She wraps her hand around the base of my erection, and *holy hell*, does it feel amazing. I let out a choked sound of surprised satisfaction as she slowly strokes me.

"Feels good?" she asks softly.

"Fuck . . . *yes*," I manage.

She leans down, and as her pink lips get closer to my cock, I close my eyes. Hell. Just the sight of her could make me come. Her tongue is soft as she runs it tentatively around the head of my cock.

I'm breathing hard, gripping the bedsheets and struggling to keep control. I've never felt so undone by a woman. She wants me—wants *this*, and that's just as hot as the feel of her sweet mouth on me.

She takes as much of me as she can, licking and sucking and stroking. I can tell from how slow she goes that she's inexperienced, and fuck if that doesn't turn me on, too. Just knowing she wants to please me is all it takes.

"Ah, *fuck* . . ." I say through gritted teeth. "I'm gonna come."

She doesn't stop, and within a few seconds, I come in her mouth, her eyes widening as she tastes it. Her lips glisten as she pulls away and gives me a questioning look.

"Baby," I say, running a hand over her hip and around to her back. "That was incredible and . . . completely unexpected."

She smiles. I sit up and kiss her softly.

"Now lie down on your back," I say.

She opens her mouth to protest, but I quiet her with a

finger over her lips. "Just do it."

No way can I let her go sleep without feeling what I just did. I don't like that she made me come first, and I plan to make up for it.

I unfasten her jeans and slide them off. Her lacy black panties are so sexy against her creamy white skin. I take my time licking the lace hems of them and kissing her thighs.

I note all the spots I kiss that make her moan softly. Inner ankles and inner thighs are her favorites. When I hook my fingers through the sides of her panties and slide them down, she closes her legs.

"Relax," I say softly.

"I haven't gotten waxed." Her voice is a low, embarrassed whisper.

I look at the dark blond curls between her legs and smile. "You look perfect."

"Really?"

"Very sexy. Now open your legs for me."

She does, and I stay on my knees, my eyes locked with hers.

"How does it feel, opening your legs when I tell you to?" I ask.

Her nipples are pebbled, and her chest rises and falls with her heavy breathing. "It feels . . . good."

"I'll never make you feel anything but good," I promise.

She gives me a lazy smile.

"I want you to flatten your hands and circle your palms gently over your nipples," I say, my cock rock hard once again.

Uncertainty only flashes across her face for an instant before she complies, her lips parting as she begins touching herself.

I can't help wrapping a hand around my renewed erection and pumping it a few times as I watch her. Damn, is she hot. I've never imagined being driven this crazy by a woman.

"Now pinch your nipples," I say. "Squeeze them between

your thumb and forefinger."

She does, and I pump my cock a few more times as she moans loudly.

"Pinch harder," I tell her.

When she does, her hips arch off the bed.

"Keep doing it," I say, bending down.

I've teased her enough. I slide my tongue into her glistening pussy, and she gasps loudly. I suck on her clit and slide a finger into her.

Oh, *hell*. She's tight. I pump my dick a few times with my free hand, imagining what it will feel like to be inside her.

Her hips are rotating, and she's breathing so hard. I push another finger in and suck harder. She cries out my name, and I feel her coming against my tongue. The sound of her saying my name does me in, and I come again, too.

When her hips fall back to the bed, she's still panting.

"Wow," is all she says.

"Tell me you liked it."

"Couldn't you tell?" she asks with a light laugh.

"Tell me anyway." I lie down on my side next to her.

"I *loved* it."

"What did you love?"

She gives me a confused look. I weave my fingers through hers.

"I want to hear you say you loved me eating your pussy."

She blushes. "I loved you . . . eating my pussy, Andrew."

"I love the taste of you. I love tasting you when you're coming. You taste so fucking good, baby."

"You do, too."

My cock twitches. I want more of her. But not tonight. The moment feels too perfect to mess with.

"You care if we sleep naked?" I ask her.

"Not at all," she says, yawning.

I kiss her one more time before we settle in away from the wet spot, her back to my chest. I pull the covers over us, feeling a rare moment of complete contentment.

Chapter Thirteen

Quinn

I'M RUNNING. IT feels more like flying, because my feet hardly touch the ground. I'm holding Bethy's hand, and she's flying behind me. There's a whooshing sound pounding through my head and the knowledge that whether I can see him or not, *he* is right behind us.

Run all you want. There's no escaping me.

He doesn't say it, but I feel it. There's no escaping. I run faster but am hit with a sick realization.

My hand isn't holding on to anything. Bethy's not there anymore.

With a horrified scream, I stop. I'm searching for her all around, but there's nothing but blackness.

"Bethy! Bethy, where are you? Bethy!" My throat burns with the force of my cries.

"Hey, it's okay," a deep, soft voice says. "Quinn, you're okay."

I suck in a breath and throw the covers away. My heart is pounding wildly.

"What?" I ask, feeling disoriented.

"Hey, it's Andrew. You were having a nightmare."

I exhale deeply, my body going slack with relief.

"Oh God, it was so real. So *real*. He was there."

"Who was there?"

Andrew brushes the hair back from my sweaty brow. I take a few breaths, steadying myself.

"No one," I say. "Just some guy we used to know in the tunnels."

"Someone who hurt you?"

My laugh is unamused. "No one ever hurt me in the tunnels. I had my knife."

He wraps an arm around my shoulder and pulls me against him. His bare chest is warm and solid. I relax for a few seconds until my temple, slick with sweat, slides across his skin.

"Sorry," I say, wiping my fingertips across my forehead to clear away the sweat.

"It's okay. You all right?"

I nod, though my heart is still racing. I glance at the clock beside Andrew's side of the bed. It's 4:21 AM.

"C'mere," Andrew says, lying down and bringing me with him. He settles me in against his chest, stroking his thumb across my bare hip in slow, lazy circles.

I've been sleeping in his bed every night for the past ten days. After that first night, it just became an unspoken thing between us. Most nights, he shows me all the ways he can bring me pleasure with his skillful hands and mouth. There was one night he was so tired he stripped his clothes off and fell asleep on his stomach as soon as he got into bed. I ran my fingers through his hair and watched him sleep until I fell asleep myself.

It's strange, this relationship we have. Last week, he passed me an envelope with ten thousand dollars in it over dinner. I miss my sister, but now that I know she's safe, I'm pretty sure I want to be here for the next four envelopes, too. Not just because of the money, but because I'm getting to know Andrew. He's private and guarded, but I'm starting to see what lies beneath that exterior.

"Want to talk about it?" he murmurs in my ear.

"No." I run my fingertips over the soft hair on his chest.

Bethy is safe. I shouldn't be upset right now, but I am. I hate that I can't escape Paul. No matter how far I run or how much time passes, he finds me in nightmares.

Slowly, my heart rate returns to normal. I'm just starting to drift back to sleep when Andrew eases himself out from under me. He works out in his upstairs gym at five thirty AM every day, no matter how late we were up the night before. And lately, we've been staying up *really* late.

"Maybe I can work out with you sometime," I say, yawning.

"Yeah? We can hit the main floor gym anytime you want."

"Why do you have two?"

"I added the one on the second level in the second stage of reno. The first-floor one was just supposed to be temporary."

"Mmm," I say in a sleepy tone.

I hear him go into his massive closet to get dressed, and I'm nearly asleep when he keys in the code on the keypad next to a door in the bedroom to go upstairs. The automatic deadbolt slides closed behind him with a dull *thunk* sound.

His bed is massive and so comfortable. The queen-size bed in my room has soft cotton sheets too, but Andrew's are all cozy and worn-in. They have the slight cedar scent of his cologne, too. I give in to the warmth and fall back asleep.

It's a little after 7 AM when I wake back up and see Andrew walking across the room. He's freshly showered, the ends of his dark hair still damp, and dressed in a navy suit with a white shirt. A striped tie is hanging around his neck, not yet tied.

"Morning," he says, his deep voice and slight smile making me wish he'd get back in bed.

"Mmm . . . good morning."

"I almost made it out of here without waking you. Go back to sleep if you can."

I sit up, keeping the covers wrapped around my bare chest. "No, I need to get up too. Those books at the library aren't gonna read themselves."

He's standing in front of a mirror tying his tie, and he looks over at me in the reflection. "Why don't you go shopping?"

I roll my eyes. "Already covered. Dawson's forcing me to go to the salon and shopping this afternoon."

"He means well."

"I know. Actually, I've been thinking."

"Yeah?"

"Do you think I'd have to get a background check to volunteer at a homeless shelter?"

Andrew turns around and meets my gaze, his tie secured in a perfect knot.

"Would a background check be an issue for you?"

I look down at the bed.

"I can help," he says. "You want me to set something up for you?"

"Could you? I mean . . . I don't have an ID, and I can't get one."

He walks over to the bed and sits down on the edge. "I'll make you a deal. I set it up, and you let Roy drive you there and home every day."

His bright blue eyes are so serious. Andrew isn't the light and happy type, but then, neither am I.

"Okay. If you're sure you can arrange it."

"I'll do it this morning. Remember, we have that reception tonight."

"I remember. It's why Dawson's making me go to the salon at three to get beautified."

Andrew gets up from the bed and glances back at me. "You couldn't possibly look any more beautiful than you do at this moment."

I smooth a hand over my messy hair and smile.

"Sadly I have an eight o'clock meeting," he says, "but I'll see you tonight."

For a second, I think he might come over and kiss me. But he just smiles and leaves. It would have been weird anyway, I'm sure. What would I have said? "Have a good day, dear?" We're not a couple or anything.

I take a shower in my own bathroom and dress in jeans and a dark green cashmere sweater. It's one Dawson picked out for me, and I have to admit, it looks really good.

After putting on some light makeup, I look at myself in the bathroom mirror. It's only been five weeks since I lived on the streets, but it feels a lifetime away. I've completely lost the dark circles under my eyes, and my collarbone doesn't stand out so prominently anymore. My hair is shinier. My breasts are back, not that they were ever big. But, still. It's been a long time since I felt confident in anything other than my survival skills. It feels good.

I bundle up and set out for the library. It's almost Thanksgiving, and Christmas decorations are starting to go up in store windows. It'll be the first Christmas Bethy and I haven't been together. I swallow the lump in my throat. Better for her to be safe and warm in Mexico than shivering in some alley with me here.

Last year, Bean got carryout Christmas dinners for us from a homeless shelter, and we ate them in an abandoned building. When Bethy and I were kids, Christmas dinner was an afterthought. Not anymore. We ate every last bite in those Styrofoam containers and loved it.

When I get to the library and settle into my chair with a

book, Anna approaches, handing over a hardback.

"Perfect color for you, dear. You look lovely."

"Thank you, Anna."

She smiles. "It's not just the sweater, though."

I smile back. "Things are going really well."

"You deserve it."

She pats my shoulder and returns to her desk. I take my coat, purse, and the two books and weave my way through the tall shelves lined with books until I'm secluded from anyone's view.

The letter is waiting for me right inside the front cover of the book. The sight of my sister's handwriting fills me with a warm sense of reassurance. I run my fingers over the letters on the envelope before carefully opening the top.

Inside the letter is a picture of Bethy. She's standing on the beach, the blue ocean and setting sun in the background. A few strands of her brown hair are blowing up in the breeze, and she's smiling. Her skin is golden with a tan.

My eyes fill with tears. She looks so healthy. So happy. For as much as I've always been the strong one, Bethy is rising to the occasion. She wants me to see that she's doing okay. I can see it in her expression. It makes me so happy I could cry.

After I stare at the photo for a few more seconds, I read the letter.

Dear Quinn,

It's so nice here. Every day is beautiful and warm. The people are all really nice, even though I don't speak the language. They help me with things and try to feed me all the time.

Bean has a job! He works with a fisherman every day, and I study with a woman named Maria. She's a teacher who had to move back home to take care of her mother who is sick. Maria is teaching me Spanish and math, and we also have reading time at the beach every day. Obviously, I like the reading time the best. It makes me think of our library.

I miss you. I can't wait until you get here and we can walk on the beach together. You'll love it. Our place is very small, but we don't need much room. There's just one bedroom, a bathroom, and a kitchen and living room combined into one. Bean sleeps on the couch, and I sleep in the bedroom. He says when you come we'll get a bigger place, but for now, we're trying not to spend much money.

Today, Maria is taking me to a farmer's market. She wants me to ask for all the food we need by name in Spanish and pay for it myself. Then we're going to cook dinner.

Here's a picture of me at the beach Maria and I go to every day. Please write me and let me know how you are. We're good, so please don't worry about us.

Love,

Bethy

I read the letter again, then place the photo back inside it and tuck it back into the envelope. Once I've stashed it safely in a pocket of my purse, I walk back to my chair and sit down to read my book for a couple hours.

Once my stomach starts grumbling, I decide it's time to go home and get lunch. After returning the books to their spots on the shelves, I slide into my coat, wrap my scarf around my face, and set back out.

My heart is so full. The buzz of energy from traffic and pedestrians surrounds me, and I realize this is my city now. This is home to me, which is funny considering I spent most of my time here hungry and desperate. But I have to say one thing for New York City—what I needed, it gave me. I had to find a place my sister and I could become invisible, and we did. And given my arrangement with Andrew, I'm even more convinced this is a city of dreams. Anything is possible here, and nothing is off-limits.

I already have a dress I want to wear to the reception tonight. It's black and beaded and very elegant. I know Andrew will love it. I'm trying to decide how to tell Dawson I don't want to go shopping for something new when a sound makes me stop in my tracks on the sidewalk.

It was a cry of pain. I'm not sure how I heard it over the sounds of traffic, but I know it was there. Where did it come from, though?

I step out of the row of pedestrians on the sidewalk to look around. It's busy and crowded everywhere. I decide I must have imagined the noise when I hear it again.

My head automatically turns toward the narrow alley the sound came from. My feet follow suit, heading into the dark, muddy space. My new shoes are sliding in the gray sludge on the ground. It's hard to see since two tall buildings block all the light, but I look from side to side as I get deeper into the alley.

And then I see it. Cowering behind a Dumpster is a very sad looking creature. Its hair is matted and filthy. Big, brown eyes look up at me, and I see the question in them: *what are you going to do to me?*

I melt. This dog needs a friend so badly. I approach him slowly, my palm up. He shrinks back against the Dumpster.

It's a wonder he's alive. He's skin and bones. As I get closer, he whimpers and I try to soothe him.

"Shh, I won't hurt you," I say softly. "You're okay."

I've almost reached him when I hear the sound of someone clearing their throat behind me.

I freeze for a second, then turn. Three men are standing just a few feet behind me. They all have on ragged coats and worn-out shoes. Their faces are weather-worn, and two of them have scraggly beards. I can see the hunger in their eyes. Whether it's for food or something else, I'm not sure.

I just know I'm in a bad situation.

"I'll take that purse," the tallest one says, eyes narrowed. "Your clothes and shoes, too."

Chapter Fourteen

Quinn

IT'S NOT THERE. I know my knife is back at the warehouse, tucked into my underwear drawer in my bedroom. But instinct sent my hand to my hip just the same.

"Your fuckin' purse," he repeats. "*Now.*"

I stand, mentally kicking myself for leaving the warehouse without my knife. But I'm resourceful. These assholes are *not* getting my letters from Bethy.

"You don't know who you're fucking with right now," I say in a steely tone. "You're not getting my purse."

I tighten my hold on the strap over my shoulder and hold the tall man's gaze. One of the men behind him laughs and takes out a handgun, holding it low and pointing it at me.

"Put it away," the tall one says without even looking at him. "You ain't shooting nobody here. Too many people close by."

He charges toward me then and shoves me against the brick wall by my shoulders. I raise a knee to his stomach, hitting just as my teeth start rattling from the impact of the wall.

After he cringes and huffs out an exhale, the man slaps me

across the face so hard it knocks the wind out of me.

"Fucker," I mutter.

He takes hold of my purse and starts pulling. I secure my arm around it as tight as I can.

"Let go, you rich bitch," he says. "You got more purses at home."

"No," I say through gritted teeth. "You can't have it."

I stomp on one of his feet, putting all my weight into it. He swears at me and rears back, punching me full in the face. I stagger back against the wall, the dark colors of the men's clothing swirling together.

Spit flies against my cheek as I scramble to keep hold of my purse. Someone is pulling on it.

"No," I cry. "No. Please. Just let me have the letters."

"You ain't gettin' shit," a voice says before laughing. The purse is wrestled away from me.

I get up but am immediately shoved back to the ground, where a hard boot to my stomach makes me howl in pain. Whoever is kicking me keeps going, hitting so hard with each blow that my whole body moves.

I think I'm being choked. Someone is pulling off my coat, and I don't even care. I taste blood. I want to breathe so badly.

Thank God Bethy's not here. She's safe. I picture her on the beach in Mexico, smiling. She's buying groceries with Maria and learning how to pronounce them in Spanish.

"Is this who we were fucking with?" a voice cackles from over me. "You should've just given us the purse, bitch."

Another kick to my stomach, and I can feel hands on the waistband of my jeans. They won't just leave me to die, then; they're going to violate me first. Pigs. Bean would gut these men and feed them their innards if he were here.

There's a loud bark, followed by another. And another.

"Shut that fuckin' dog up," one of the men mutters.

"Let's get out of here, Tony. We got the purse."

The dog is still barking, over and over. I hear gravel flying as the men run away. Finally, I suck in a few breaths of air, though it hurts.

"Thank you," I whisper to the dog. "Thank you."

He's still barking. I pull myself into a sitting position just as a man's voice calls out, "Hey! Is everything okay?"

"No," I say, my voice coming out a croak. "Help, please."

A figure comes closer. He's middle-aged, with a thick waistline and a rumpled suit.

"Oh, Christ," he says when he sees me. "I'll call 911."

"No," I say frantically. "No, please don't."

I want to get up and walk back to the warehouse, but I can't. It's about a mile away, and I just can't do it.

"I'm okay," I say. "I just . . . I want to go home. It's not far. About a mile. Can you hail a cab and ask if I can have someone pay for it over the phone?"

"Here," the man says, leaning down to me. His scuffed black dress shoes are now stuck in an inch of mud. "My name's Jim. I'm gonna help you up and get you home, okay? I've got the cab fare."

My eyes fill with tears as he reaches for my waist. "No. Please . . . not there. It hurts so bad."

"What can I do?" he asks.

"Can you give me your arm? If I can pull myself up on it, I think I can get up."

"Sure." He holds out his arm and I clutch it, forcing myself not to cry out from the pain all over as I get into a hunched over standing position.

I look down at myself. I'm wearing a mud-splattered white camisole, which I had on under the sweater that came off with my coat. My jeans are pulled halfway down my thighs. I have no shoes. Bastards took my coat, shoes, and cashmere sweater.

Cringing, I pull up my jeans and button them.

"I think we should call the police," Jim says. "Were you . . . assaulted?"

"I just want to go home." I look over at the dog, back in his spot next to the Dumpster. "Can you pick him up and carry him for me?"

"You want to take that thing home? Is it yours?"

"He is now."

Jim shrugs and picks up the dog, who is visibly shaking.

"I'll repay you for this," I promise Jim on the slow walk out of the alley. "For your suit and the cab fare and everything."

He shakes his head. "It's okay. I got a wife and two sisters. I hope somebody would stop to help them if they needed it. I'm just sorry I didn't get here sooner."

Jim wouldn't have been much help against the three thugs, but I smile with gratitude anyway. We draw a few stares as he hails a cab. I've got blood and mud all over me, and he's holding a dog that looks like it belongs in an ASPCA ad.

"I'll give you some extra for the mess," Jim promises the cabbie who pulls up and gives us a skeptical look.

"Meatpacking District," I say, grimacing from the pain of getting into the car. "I don't know the address, but I can get you there."

The cabbie just shakes his head and drives. I direct him, feeling a wave of relief as the warehouse comes into view. The cab pulls up out front, and Jim gets out, still holding the shaking dog. I slide out after him.

"Can you carry the dog to the front door for me?" I ask.

"Sure thing." Jim gestures to the cabbie to wait, and he follows me. I don't even make it to the front steps that lead to the door before two men in dark suits walk over briskly to stop me.

"Miss Jones," one of them says, "what happened?"

I furrow my brow and stay silent.

"We're part of Mr. Wentworth's security team," he says. "Who is this man?"

They look at Jim.

"I was attacked," I explain. "He helped me. Got me the cab to get home."

"Let's get you inside," the man in the suit with short dark hair says.

The other one is thanking Jim and taking the dog, which makes me smile. He looks unfazed by the mud-covered beast ruining his nice suit.

"Jim, thank you," I say, turning. "Thank you so much."

He nods, smiles, and walks back to the cab. The other security guard follows us up the steps, where he keys in a code to open the front door.

"Turner!" the dark-haired guard calls as we walk into the open living room.

"Hmm?" Andrew's housekeeper and cook sticks her head around a corner and sees us. "Oh, sweet Jesus! What happened?"

She runs toward me.

"I'll phone Mr. Wentworth," one of the guards says.

"Let's run a full property sweep," the other one says. "Just to be safe."

Turner leads me into Andrew's bathroom, where she looks me over from head to toe.

"Girl, what happened?" she asks, her big, dark eyes swimming with concern.

"I was mugged," I say miserably. "Three guys took my purse and my sweater and shoes."

She shakes her head with disgust. "Thug bastards. You're a mess, girl. I think we need to get you to a hospital."

"No. I think it looks worse than it is. Can you just help me clean up?"

"'Course I can."

I remember the picture of Bethy that was in my purse, and my eyes flood with tears. I want to hold them back, but I can't. Her precious letters are gone. I bury my face in my hands and cry angry tears.

"I'm gonna make you some of that chai tea you like," Turner says softly. "You just sit here."

She leaves and I try to get ahold of myself, but I just can't. It's all hitting me at once: the beating, the fear, the near-sexual assault, the dog, my letters . . .

I cry until I have snot running down my face, and when I hear someone walk through the bathroom door, it's not Turner, but Andrew. He's breathing hard, and his forehead is soaked with sweat.

"Quinn!" He drops to his knees in front of me. "What the hell happened? Are you okay?"

"I was . . . mugged," I say, trying to sniff away more snot.

Andrew takes out a cloth handkerchief and gives it to me. I wipe my nose, cringing when I see the bloodstained handkerchief.

"You can dock my pay for that," I say, trying to laugh. But I can't.

"Stop it. Are you okay?"

I nod. "I think so. I was walking home, and I heard a crying sound. There was a dog in an alley, and I was trying to approach him when three dickless thugs jumped me from behind."

"Three men?"

"They wanted my purse, but I wouldn't give it to them."

Andrew's eyes widen. "Quinn . . . it's replaceable. You are not."

The tears are welling in my eyes again. "But Bethy's letters . . . and her picture, they aren't replaceable. They're gone. I don't have her address and she wanted me to write her back, but I can't now."

I'm crying again. Andrew sighs softly.

"Your sister."

"Yes," I whisper.

"I'm so sorry." He closes his eyes for a second. "What did they do to you?"

I shrug. "Just your typical mugging. Punched, kicked, pushed . . . and I think choked."

Andrew's jaw tightens. "Fucking cowards. What about your clothes? Did they . . . ?"

"No. Almost." I laugh through my tears. "Guess who saved me?"

His brow furrows with confusion. "The guy who brought you home?"

"The dog. He barked and barked until the guys got scared of being caught and ran. And then he barked until help came."

"Smart dog."

"I'm keeping him," I say. "And if you don't want him here . . . I understand, but I won't be able to stay, either."

"Relax, Quinn. The dog can stay, okay?" He takes my hand and brings it to his lips, kissing my knuckles. "I'm so sorry you're hurt."

"You got here really fast."

"Roy was driving me here but we got stuck in traffic, so I ran the last two miles."

"In your suit?"

"Yeah."

I smile at him. "I'd hug you if I wasn't such a mess."

He reaches for me. He's on his knees on the bathroom floor, and I'm sitting on the edge of the bathtub. I sink against him and close my eyes.

"You're okay now," he says softly.

"Turner said she'll help me clean up, but . . . can you help me instead?"

Andrew has seen all of me, and I'm more comfortable with him than Turner. I also just want to be near him right now.

"I would but . . . I have to go take care of something," he says.

I lean back and meet his gaze. "Oh. You mean work?"

He shakes his head. "I'll be back in a little while. My security team is on alert, and I promise you are completely safe here."

"But . . . you're leaving?"

He kisses the back of my hand and stands up. "I have to. I'm calling Ty to come over and look at you."

I nod and swallow hard. I don't want him to go. Andrew is the comfort I need right now. But what can I say?

"You have to go?" I ask.

"I do. I'll be back as soon as I can, okay?"

"Yeah. Okay."

He walks out of the bathroom, and a couple minutes later, Turner walks in with a mug of chai tea and a stack of fresh clothes. She helps me take a shower and dress in yoga pants and a T-shirt. I try not to think about Andrew the entire time, but I can't help it.

Why would he run two miles to get here and then leave within a few minutes? Doesn't he know how much I need him right now?

Ty arrives right after Turner settles me into Andrew's bed. Like Andrew, he's ridiculously handsome. Blond, blue-eyed, and tall, he has a contagious smile.

"Let's have a look," he says kindly, checking over my stomach, neck, and face. I hope he doesn't ask any questions about Andrew and me, because I'm too emotionally fragile to think of a good cover story right now.

"Can you look at the dog, too?" I ask as he presses on my stomach gingerly. "Ow, that hurts."

"Yeah, I'll take him to an animal hospital," Ty says.

"You don't have to do that."

"Sure I do. He's important to you, and you're important to Andrew."

My heart pounds faster. *Am* I important to Andrew? Am I any more important than anyone else on his payroll?

"You're lucky," Ty says. "Bruised ribs for sure, and you'll be sore for a few days. But I don't think it's anything more than that. I'll need to run blood work today and again tomorrow because we want to make sure none of your internal organs are damaged."

"Okay. Thank you."

"I'm prescribing some pain medicine. You'll need it."

I sit back against the pillows and nod. Ty takes a syringe and a small bottle from his medical bag.

"Would you like something to help you rest?" he asks.

"No. Thanks, but no."

"Okay. You guys call me if you need anything at all, okay? Anything. I'll text Andrew when I get the dog taken care of. I guarantee they'll admit him. He's not in good shape."

"Don't let them put him down," I say, my voice shaking. "I don't want that. He saved me."

Ty pats my hand reassuringly. "I'll treat him like he's my own, Quinn. I promise."

He leaves, and I lie back on the pillows Turner fluffed up behind me. Where is Andrew?

The reception. I sigh as I realize he probably went to that reception we were supposed to go to together. The thought of Dahlia hitting on him again makes me irrationally angry. I'm not thrilled with Andrew right now, but still. He'd better manage to fend her off without my help this time.

I cry about the letters some more and try to commit Bethy's photo to memory. If karma is a thing, I'll see those assholes again, and I'll have my knife next time.

Afternoon turns into evening, and the bedroom is dark

when Andrew pushes the door open. I'd almost drifted to sleep, but I sit up when I see his broad-shouldered silhouette in the doorway.

"Andrew?"

"Hey," he says softly. He walks into the room, and I turn on the nightstand lamp so I can see him as he approaches the bed.

It can't be. It can't possibly fucking *be*. But it is.

My mouth falls open in shock as he holds out the black bag to me. I recognize it immediately.

It's my fucking purse.

Chapter Fifteen

Andrew

SHE GRABS THE large black purse and throws it open, digging into a pocket. When she pulls a couple envelopes from inside, her eyes widen and fill with tears.

"What is this?" she demands. "What . . . how?"

I sit down on the side of the bed. "The how doesn't matter. You wanted it, and I got it."

She scoots to the side of the bed and slips out of it, wincing from the pain. "The how *does* matter, Andrew. It matters a fucking lot." She holds the letters up in the air. "How did you do this?"

"Hey, you need to be in bed."

"Answer me," she says, her eyes pooling with emotion. "Because right now I feel really violated."

"*Violated*?" I stand up and face her. This is not the reaction I was expecting. I thought she'd be thrilled to have her sister's letters back.

"You just *happened* to find the men who robbed me in the largest city in the world? How fucking stupid do you think I am?"

"Quinn, look—"

"No, *you* look." She approaches me and points at my face. "Explain yourself."

I sigh deeply. "I can't."

"You mean *won't*."

"No, I *can't*."

"Andrew—"

"Where are you from? Why'd you send Bethy away? Why don't you have any ID?"

Her nostrils flare with anger. "You know I can't tell you any of that."

"*Won't*," I say firmly. "Same fucking difference, Quinn."

"What is this?" she yells. "Is this some mind game you're playing with me? You want to get my story so you . . . what? What the hell did you *do*, Andrew?"

"I got your letters back. That's what you wanted. How about a thank-you?"

"Thank you? You can't possibly think I'm this stupid."

I roll my eyes, exasperated. One of those assholes who mugged her hit me in the stomach and I'm sore. Definitely not up for a fight.

"We both have secrets, Quinn," I remind her. "And the how behind *this*—" I point at her purse on the bed "—is one of mine."

"You hired them." Her accusing tone makes me flinch.

"Are you fucking serious?" I roar, not caring who hears me.

"You set it up so you could save the day. Maybe they got out of hand with the beating, I don't know."

I step back, feeling wound so tight I could explode. "That is the craziest shit I've ever heard. You think I'd do that?"

"There's no other rational explanation for how you got my purse back. None. If I'm wrong, please tell me. You have no idea how much I want to be wrong right now."

"You're wrong."

"Then *how*?"

"I don't answer to you," I remind her. "I've done every possible thing I can think of to make you happy since you got here, and I tried to do that again. You were crying. They hurt you. I did what needed to be done. Can't you just leave it at that?"

She just looks at me, and the answer is in her eyes. I see doubt there and the return of the hard, steely gaze from the first night we met.

"I'd never hurt you," I say, taking a step closer to her. "And I'd never let anyone else hurt you, either."

A purple bruise marks her cheek, and her lip is swollen. I hate what happened to her today. The deep, burning anger I feel for the men who touched her is familiar to me. I felt it after 9/11, when I lost my father. That kind of anger is dangerous without an outlet. Making those three thugs sorry and getting Quinn's letters back had been my only option.

She swallows hard and looks at the ground. "Thank you. I'll sleep in my room."

And when she walks out of the room, she takes everything we've built with her. The familiarity, the closeness, the *trust* . . . gone.

I unknowingly ruined everything. But I know if I could do it over, I wouldn't change a thing. I can't sit by while men like those assholes get away with hurting Quinn. She's been hurt by too many people.

I go into the bathroom for a long, hot shower. I want her in my bed tonight, so much. She could have another nightmare. God knows she's got plenty of reasons to.

I already knew her sister's name. It's the name she screams during the nightmares. Bethy is everything to Quinn. I can hear the terror in her voice when she says her name.

When I get out of the shower, I dress in clean underwear

and a T-shirt and climb into bed. No reason to sleep naked without Quinn next to me. I already miss the feel of her warm, slight body next to mine.

I stare at the ceiling, worries shooting rapid-fire in my mind. The biggest one is that Quinn will leave. She'll just slip away without warning to escape me because she's afraid of me now.

If she does, I could find her. Just as easily as I could figure out who she really is if I wanted to. She has no idea I'm one of the hardest people in the world to keep her kind of secrets from.

I wouldn't, though. If she goes, I'll have to bear it and remember that being close to someone is impossible for me. It was only a matter of time, anyway. But I was really hoping the time wasn't this close.

Chapter Sixteen

Quinn

THE SECURITY GUARDS are named Steve and Micah. I've seen them often in the four days since the attack because every time I try to leave the house alone, one of them follows me. They don't even try to be discreet about it.

I'd complain to Andrew, but I'm still not speaking to him. If he asks me a question, I reply, but that's it. I'm dreading Thursday, when we're going to his mother's house for Thanksgiving. My face is still purple and yellow with bruising, which I'm sure won't escape her notice.

As I walk past Micah in the warehouse's parking garage, he puts on his dark, stocking beanie, preparing to follow me.

"It's okay, I'm riding with Roy," I say.

"Mr. Wentworth said you're starting volunteer work at the homeless shelter today, and he wants me to go with you."

I lower my brows. "Go with me? Why?"

"Just to be safe."

"This is ridiculous. I have my knife." I pull open the new winter parka Dawson bought me. My knife is strapped to my thigh again, where it should have been all along.

"I'm just following orders, ma'am," Micah says.

I shake my head. "So I have to show up at a homeless shelter in an Escalade with a driver and a security guard?"

"Sorry."

"It's fine," I say with a sigh. "Just get in."

"Morning, Miss Jones," Roy says as he opens my door. I wonder if Andrew's staff realizes my last name is *not* Jones.

On the ride to the shelter, I open the manila envelope Andrew left on the kitchen island this morning. There's a birth certificate and driver's license inside with the name Susanna Hopkins. The photo on the driver's license is mine. I inhale sharply as I look at it, wondering how the hell Andrew did this.

Money can buy a lot, but this? I decide not to overthink it. This driver's license is a ticket to freedom for me. I need to do more than sit around the empty warehouse and library all the time. At the shelter, I can meet people facing the struggles I know all too well. I can do something that matters.

Roy drops me off in front of the Helping Hands shelter, and Micah follows me inside. It's small but bright and clean. Photos of smiling people line the walls. A receptionist asks for my name, and as soon as I tell her I'm Susanna Hopkins, a man wearing jeans and a flannel comes out to shake my hand.

"Pete Larsen," he says with a grin. "I'm the executive director here. I can't thank you enough for your donation, Miss Hopkins. It's going to make a huge difference in a lot of lives."

"Donation?"

"Mr. Wentworth made it on behalf of both of you. He said you'd like to volunteer as well, which is great. We can always use the help."

I feel a warm affection for Andrew until I remember how upset I am with him. I think constantly about how he could have gotten my purse back without having anything to do with the mugging, and I come up empty every time.

"Just let me know what I can do," I say. "And my friend Micah came along to help, too."

"As long as we can work together, I'm game," Micah says.

Pete assigns us to the kitchen, where we peel potatoes and carrots. We help serve soup and sandwiches for lunch, and I feel a pang for every young child whose plate and bowl I fill. Their big eyes and warm smiles remind me so much of Bethy.

It's a good day, and when Pete asks if we can come back later this week to help serve Thanksgiving dinner, I hate to say no. I'd rather be here than spend an uncomfortable day with Andrew and his mother.

I appreciate what Andrew did for the shelter, so I smile at him when he comes into the kitchen after work.

"You had a good day?" he asks, taking off his dark red tie.

"Yes. Thank you for giving to the shelter."

"Of course. Charitable contributions are a tax write-off."

"How much did you donate?"

"Two fifty."

My lips part with surprise. "You mean . . . $250,000?"

"Yes. Is dinner ready?"

I come from a family with money, but I don't think it's the kind of wealth Andrew has. He can buy anything he wants. And yet, I wonder if he understands the power of that. Does he know that the money he gave to the shelter was a lot more than just a tax deduction?

"Turner left the roaster set on warm so we could eat when you got here," I say.

Before the attack, we would have talked over dinner. I would ask him how work was, and he would explain whatever real estate deal he was working on. I'd tell him about the books I'd read at the library that day, and he'd pretend to be interested.

Instead, we eat in silence. When we're finished, I move the dishes to the counter by the sink and start unloading clean dishes from the dishwasher.

"Leave that for Turner," Andrew says.

"I've got it."

"This is what I pay her for."

"You're paying me, too," I remind him.

"Not for this."

My hand stops over the glass I was about to take out of the dishwasher. It's true. He's paying me a lot of money, and I'm not earning it.

"What would you like from me?" I ask, not turning around.

I hear him walking across the wood floor toward me. His hands settle lightly on my waist, and I feel the heat of his large frame behind me.

"I'd like it to be like it was," he says. "When we were getting closer. When you trusted me with your body."

"It's not really like that, though," I say softly. "You can have whatever you want from me physically, trust or not."

He exhales his frustration. "Is that how it's gonna be, then? I have to command sexual favors from you?"

I turn and look up at him. "They're not favors. This is our deal, Andrew."

"It can be good for *both* of us," he says, his hands tightening around my hips. "Just let go and enjoy it like you did before. I'll give you anything you want."

It feels good, having his hands on me again. That's some messed-up shit right there. I'm angry at him, I don't trust him, but the attraction is stronger than ever. It's like he flipped a switch inside me, and I don't know how to turn it off.

He doesn't have to know, though. Maybe I can't control how my body responds to him, but I can control what I do about it.

"You tell *me* what *you* want," I say, forcing myself to hold his gaze. "I work for you, remember? So just say it, and it's yours."

His nostrils flare slightly. "You don't mean that."

"Try me."

His fist tightens around a handful of the front of my shirt, and he pulls me to him, *hard*. I inhale sharply as my hips bump against his muscled thighs.

"I'm a very controlling man, Quinn," he says in a low tone.

"Really? I hadn't noticed," I say, intending it to come out sarcastic. Instead, it sounds breathy and a little desperate.

"You haven't seen that side of me, but I'll damn well show it to you if you're asking me to."

"That's how you like it, isn't it? You give the orders and cut the checks, and everyone does exactly as you say?"

"I do like that, yes." He leans down so his mouth is just an inch above mine. I feel his warm breath on my lips, and my body heats in response.

He's going to kiss me. I'm going to like it. But he doesn't have to know it.

"Strip for me," he says. "Everything off but your bra. Then bend over the kitchen counter and give me a nice view of your gorgeous ass."

I force myself not to let my shock show. "Strip?"

"Ask and it's mine, right?" His lips curve in just a hint of a smile.

Asshole. He wants to make me eat my words. It won't work.

"You got it, boss," I say, stepping out of his hold on me.

I take a steadying breath as I walk across the large kitchen to a counter a safe distance from Andrew. Safe for him or safe for me, I'm not sure.

I toy with the hem of my shirt, my heart racing. And then I realize it may not just be Andrew watching me right now.

"Are there cameras in here?" I ask.

"No. Not in this room."

"Where, then?" There's a note of panic in my voice. "In the bedroom?"

Andrew shakes his head. "I'd never do that to you. There are cameras in certain rooms, but nothing's being recorded now."

"When do they record?"

"Only when I want them to, which is rare. They're in rooms like my office and the living room, nothing private." He leans back against the counter, and I can swear I almost see him smirking. "Now on with my show."

It's only skin, I remind myself. I'm just flashing some skin for the man.

Unless he decides he wants more . . .

I slip off my socks and pull the shirt up and off over my head. If I was supposed to tease him by making it slow and sexy, I failed. But he seems to be enjoying the view of my breasts in a lacy turquoise bra.

My eyes stay locked on his as I unbutton my jeans and wiggle my hips to slide them down. His gaze is dark and intense, and his hands grip the counter he's standing in front of.

With way more wiggling than needed, I get the jeans off. He's a very controlling man, as he said. But right now, I feel like the one with the power. His dark blue eyes seem to be telling me he couldn't look away if he wanted to.

I give him a sultry smile and then turn around and shake my ass just a little as I slide the panties down slowly. I hear his deep exhale as I reach my thighs and let them fall to the floor.

Bend over, he said. *Give me a nice view.* I steady myself with my hands on the counter and bend down.

"Oh, shit," he mutters softly. "Yeah. Raise that ass in the air for me."

I can feel his gaze on my bare skin. I should be cold as I stand here naked in the kitchen, but I'm warm all over. His approaching footsteps make me shiver with awareness.

"So sexy," he says from behind me. He touches a single fingertip to my spine and runs it down, making me moan softly.

"You don't have to admit how much you like it, baby," he says. "I already know."

I'm trying to think of a snarky comeback when I feel his fingertips at my wet entrance, sliding back and forth. I let out a shaky gasp because I have to. It feels too good to deny.

It's all I can do to hold on as he puts two fingers inside me, groaning as they slide in easily. He's rubbing my bare ass with his other hand.

My body doesn't care how pissed I am at him or whether he lied to me or even if he's a good guy. I'm pushing my hips back against his fingers, only thinking of wanting more, more, more.

When he bends to my ass cheek and gives it a soft bite, followed by a kiss, I let out a long, loud wail as I come on his hand. It's primal. Andrew can manipulate my body to meet his will, and we both know it.

He slows his fingers, only stopping when my body goes limp against the counter. He presses a soft kiss to my shoulder.

"You were right, baby," he says against my skin. "I do love giving you orders. Let's do this again soon."

I can't look at him right now. I know what I'll see on his face: smug, satisfied victory.

And why does that piss me off? I can't deny his victory feels pretty damn amazing. But we both know he proved his point—his control over me isn't just something I allow begrudgingly. It's something that, at times, I actually crave. When Andrew looks at me with lust in his eyes, I'm powerless to fight what it does to me.

Chapter Seventeen

Quinn

THE PAST FEW days have made me question a lot of things. Mostly I'm wondering just how much of myself I'm selling to Andrew here.

I just keep wondering . . . Why do I stay here when I suspect he set up the mugging just so he could play hero? Is it only for the money? How did I survive more than four years on the streets with little more than a scratch, only to let my guard down so hard I could have been beaten to death or raped in that alley? Did I already have this sexual hunger lying dormant inside me, or did *he* create it?

I consider these things and always come back to thoughts of Andrew. He takes me to bed every night, and we push our boundaries a little further each time. I'm surprisingly eager for him to take things all the way. His cool demeanor, powerful frame, and piercing blue eyes have gotten to me. I'm feeling something for him.

Never did I think I'd develop feelings for a rich man who exudes such power and control. It reminds me too much of the man I'm running from.

"You'll pay for that, you little bitch." His evil laugh rumbles. "Run all you want. There's no escaping me."

I'm sitting in Andrew's library, lost in thought rather than the open book on my lap, when I hear male voices in the other room.

I get up and walk that way and find Steve, the security guy, talking to a man in jeans and a T-shirt.

"Everything okay?" Steve asks me.

"Yeah, I'm good."

I walk into the kitchen to get some water. Turner is there, chopping vegetables for the dinner she's making.

"How you doin', girl?" she asks.

"Pretty good." I slide onto a barstool at the breakfast bar and open my water. "How about you?"

"Can't complain," she says with a smile. "My baby's graduating from high school soon. I'm in party planning mode."

"That's great. Son or daughter?"

"Daughter. Jaqueline. I have two boys too, but they're younger."

"She's graduating at this time of year?"

Turner smiles. "A semester early. Starting at NYU next semester."

"Wow. You must be so proud of her."

"I sure am."

"So . . . need some help with that? I'm pretty good with a knife."

Not that I've used the kind she's using much, but still. I'm eager to spend time with her. Turner is warm and happy. She's the kind of mom I wish I had.

She passes me a cutting board, a knife, and some carrots, and I get to work. I can hear Steve talking to the guy in the other room about some sort of installation work.

"What's he doing?" I ask Turner in a low tone.

She shrugs. "Some sort of wire installation, I think."

We're making vegetable beef stew, and it's starting to smell really good by the time we finish cleaning up and Turner puts on her coat and gets her purse.

"See you tomorrow," she says, giving me a wink as she heads for the front door.

"Hey," the installation guy says to me with a wave. He looks like he's in his twenties. He's blond and fit, with tattoos on his arms.

"Hey."

"Do you by chance know where the server room is in this place?" he asks.

"Server? I have no idea."

"That's okay. I can wait 'til Andrew gets home." His gaze flicks to mine. "I'm Greg, by the way."

"Nice to meet you." I smile but don't tell him my name. Old habits die hard.

I hear footsteps behind me, and when I turn, I see Andrew. He's loosening his tie and giving me a look that's definitely not happy. He walks past me without saying a word.

"How's it going, Greg?" he asks with an edge.

"I'm about done for the day. I need to get into your server room tomorrow."

"It's not accessible. If you give me instructions, I can handle the work in there."

Greg furrows his brow. "Not accessible? How will you reach it, then?"

"I mean it's not accessible to *you*. No one but me goes in there."

"Uh . . . okay. I can try to write down some instructions."

"Whatever it is, it won't be a problem. I've got a computer engineering degree."

Greg nods and packs up his tools. "All right, man. Be back

tomorrow."

"Check in with security again."

"Got it."

Greg leaves, and Andrew walks back into the kitchen.

"You're feeling pretty fucking friendly tonight," he says, meeting my eyes.

I shrug. "Just being nice."

"You're not that nice to *me*."

I can't help giving him a pointed look. "I deep throat you on command. What's nicer than that, Andrew?"

Within seconds, he's in front of me, his big, imposing presence making me want to take a step back. He holds on to my shoulders, his gaze burning me with its intensity. On the streets, this is when I'd push him away and pull out my knife.

"Did he spend thousands on new clothes for you?" Andrew demands. "Would he give you anything you ask for? "

I cut in. "I don't ask you for *anything*."

"That's your fucking loss, Quinn, because I'd make it happen. I can't believe you have the *audacity* to smile at another man like that."

His massive hands on me make me feel put off and turned on at the same time. I hold his gaze, because I'm not backing down.

"I *smiled*. Stop being such an asshole about it."

He leans in, his eyes narrowing. "You don't smile at me like that. Why the fuck not? Is it his looks? Do blond guys make you wet?"

I narrow my eyes in return. "No. It's because he looked at me like a *person* instead of a *thing*."

Silence hangs between us for a few seconds. He lets go of me, hurt pooling in his eyes.

"That's what you think? You think you're a *thing* to me?"

"Sometimes. I don't know, Andrew. I am on your payroll."

He narrows his eyes. "And that means I don't care about you?"

"I don't know what it means. I don't understand you."

"The feeling's mutual."

This is the Andrew I have no control over. When he's like this, he's the boss. I want to make him smile, even now. I want to make him groan with pleasure. I want his naked, warm body wrapped protectively around mine as he kisses my shoulder. It's those times that *I'm* the one in charge.

He looks away and runs a hand through his thick, dark hair. It's sticking up a little when he's done, reminding me of the way he looks when we wake up in the morning.

"You want some dinner?" he asks.

"Okay."

We eat in strained silence, and he doesn't even bitch when I do the dishes. Then he disappears into his home office for the night, and once again, I'm alone.

Chapter Eighteen

Andrew

DAWSON'S BROW IS furrowed as he stops in the open doorway of my home office on Thanksgiving morning.

"My door code doesn't work anymore," he says shortly.

"Yeah," I say absently. "The security guys reset everything after Quinn was attacked."

"I'll need a new code."

I look up from my desk. He's leaning against the doorframe with his arms crossed. He's seemed off lately, but I can't put my finger on why.

"No one's getting codes for now. My security team has someone out front around the clock, so they'll let you in."

He shakes his head almost imperceptibly. "I'm locked out now?"

"Everyone is."

"Even Quinn?"

"For now. It's for her safety. She always has a security guard with her when she leaves anyway, so they make sure she gets back inside safely."

Dawson walks in, closing the door behind him and sitting down in the leather club chair in front of my desk.

"Don't you trust me?" he asks.

"It's not about trust." I fold the letter I was writing and put it in an envelope. "It's about security. If Quinn's here, I need to know no one can get inside without going through security."

"She must've honed some serious skills on the streets," Dawson mutters.

"What the fuck is that supposed to mean?"

He shrugs. "I've never seen you this way over a woman. I don't get it. It's gotta be about the way she sucks your rod."

I sit forward in my chair, trying to rein in the anger that wants to propel me across the desk right now.

"I don't pay you to speculate on any aspect of my life," I say in a measured tone. "You are my assistant. Do your fucking work and keep your mouth shut. Are we clear?"

"Of course," he says sheepishly. "I apologize."

I narrow my eyes at him. "Don't be an asshole to Quinn, Dawson. I'll fire your ass so fast you won't know what hit you. Treat her like a queen. Same goes for the dog."

"The dog?"

"It's at an animal hospital now, but she's keeping it. She was trying to help the dog when she was attacked, and she says he ended up saving her."

There's a beat of silence before he says, "Okay. I can go pick up some dog supplies now."

I open one of my desk drawers and reach into an envelope of cash, taking out five one hundred dollar bills and adding them into the envelope with the letter.

"Not today," I say. "It's a holiday. Take tomorrow and the weekend off, too. There is just one thing I'd like you to do this morning, though."

"Sure."

I slide the envelope with the letter and money across my desk and then pass him a business card. "My security guy Steve got this card from the guy who helped Quinn the other day. I need you to call him and deliver this to him."

Dawson takes the envelope and nods. "I'll take care of it."

"Thanks."

He leaves without another word. I glance at my watch and sigh deeply. Time to go to my mom's. Things are already tense between Quinn and me, and this won't help. But it's a holiday, so I have to suck it up.

Quinn is reading something on her phone and smiling when I walk into the kitchen. She looks so pretty with her hair loose around her shoulders. Something inside me shifts, and I realize I need things to be good between us again. I don't just want to see her smiling; I want to *make* her smile.

"I just talked to someone at the animal hospital," she says. "The dog can come home tomorrow."

"That's good. I gave Roy the day off, so I'll take you to get him."

She nods silently.

"How was the shelter yesterday?" I ask, pouring myself a cup of coffee from the pot on the counter. I'd worked so late last night that Quinn had already been asleep when I got home.

"It was good." She tucks her blond hair behind one ear. "Hey, can I ask you a question?"

"Yeah."

"How did you get me that fake driver's license? And birth certificate? There was even a passport in that envelope. How is that possible?"

"I've got connections."

"Yeah, but . . . *legal* ones?

"Ah . . . not exactly. But I got you what you needed, didn't I?"

"You did. But . . ." She looks away.

"What?"

She sighs softly and looks back at me. "Was it the same people who helped you with the purse thing?"

"The purse thing?"

Her expression is exasperated. "How could you have gotten my purse back if you didn't know who took it?"

I glance at my wristwatch. "Can we talk about this on the way?"

"Sure."

"You look really nice, by the way."

She's wearing a dark orange dress with brown leggings and tall brown leather boots. Even all covered up, she looks sexy.

"Thanks. I picked this out myself."

"You know, I sent Dawson with you for that first shopping trip because I figured you'd be overwhelmed. But you don't need him anymore. I'll tell him to back off."

"I'd appreciate that."

I take both our coats from the hooks hanging off the kitchen and hand hers to her. Then I lead the way to the elevator and stand aside as she gets on. Being so close to her makes me want her even more than usual. When I slide my arm around her waist, I feel her tense.

"What's wrong?" I ask.

"I want to finish our conversation. About my purse."

I drop my hand from her waist. "Like I said, I have connections. And one of the reasons I have them is because I keep the relationships confidential. Why can't you trust me? I've never done anything but look out for you."

The elevator doors open and we step off. I turn to Quinn, my voice echoing slightly in the underground parking garage.

"I trust *you*," I remind her. "I know almost nothing about you, and what I do know could be interpreted as incriminating.

You can't get ID, you won't tell me your real name, and you're paranoid about anyone taking photos of us that could be published. For all I know, I could be harboring a fugitive. But I see something in your eyes, Quinn, and I hear something in your voice, and it tells me to trust you. My instincts are never wrong. What do your instincts tell you about me?"

Her smile is soft, relaxed. "That you're not a bad person, and you want me to be happy here. That you keep everyone an arm's length and not just me."

"That's true. You were so upset about the letters, and I just wanted to get them back for you."

She nods. "And I never thanked you."

"You yelled at me and called me an asshole," I say with a shrug. "Close enough."

"I shouldn't have accused you of setting up the mugging. I guess I never considered there could be a good reason you didn't want me to know how you got my purse back."

I reach over to stroke my thumb across her jawline. "I need to apologize for being an asshole to you. I sometimes don't handle frustration well."

"Sometimes?" She gives me an amused smile.

I lean down to kiss her forehead. "That's right, sometimes. And you're the same way."

"Me?"

I tip her chin up with my thumb, stemming another argument with a kiss. Quinn holds on to the sides of my coat, pulling on them as I kiss her deeper. I can feel the difference in this kiss and the ones we shared when she was mad at me. I felt her fire for me then, but it was all physical. She's opening herself back up to me, and I wish like hell we could spend this day alone together.

My mother's waiting, though. Reluctantly, I pull away from Quinn.

"We need to go," she says.

"Yeah."

I want to let her know what she's in for as we drive to my mother's penthouse apartment.

"So, Thanksgiving at my mom's house is pretty . . . upscale," I say.

"Upscale?" She turns to me with a questioning look.

"Like crystal and cloth napkins. It's not like the Thanksgivings you see on TV with big families hugging each other and playing board games while eating pie out of the container."

"I'm mentally canceling my plan to hug your mother and break Yahtzee out of my purse."

My laugh holds a note of tension. "I guess you've met my mother, so you know she's not the warmest."

"My mother isn't, either."

"Tell me something about your mom."

She considers for a few seconds before answering. "She sees what she wants to see. Like when my dad was dying, she refused to believe he wouldn't pull through, even at the very end when the doctors told her there was no hope."

"That was hard for you." I can tell by her forlorn expression that it was.

"Yes. I was just a kid, and my dad was telling me his last wishes because my mom refused to listen."

Traffic is bumper-to-bumper in the city due to the big Thanksgiving parade. We'll have a long drive to my mom's. I'm glad for the time alone with Quinn.

"As hard as it was to lose my dad like I did, with no warning, I can't imagine what knowing he was going to die would have been like."

"Grueling," she says softly. "Painful. But I'm grateful I got to have those talks with him at the end. I think it helped me when he passed away."

My throat is tight with emotion. I clear my throat before speaking again.

"I still sometimes dream about talking to my dad. It was all the time when I was a kid. I'd give up everything I have for just five more minutes with my dad."

"He'd be proud of you," she says softly.

I take a deep breath and creep ahead in the long line of cars. "Tell me about a good memory with your mom."

Quinn smiles and leans her head back against the headrest. "We used to bake cookies together. I loved that. What about you—any happy memories with your mom?"

"Yeah, lots of 'em. I was all she had after dad died. She never had any interest in remarrying. We used to go to Martha's Vineyard every summer and spend two weeks doing nothing. Just watching movies and walking and eating out."

"It's hard for me to picture your mom relaxing."

I laugh at that. "Yeah, I know."

Traffic finally picks up, and we make it to my mom's place. I'm planning to keep Quinn by my side all day so she doesn't end up getting drilled with questions by my mom.

I park in the garage, and Quinn reaches for my hand on the elevator ride up. She's nervous. I am, too. I've never brought a woman home like this.

I key in the code to Mom's apartment, which I had set up with a security system like mine. We walk inside and find Mom's friend Gloria and two other couples are drinking white wine with Mom in the main living room.

"Andrew," Mom says, coming over to give me a hug, "and you brought your friend."

She turns to look at Quinn. "My God, what happened?"

"She was mugged," I say, wrapping an arm around Quinn's waist.

"*Mugged*?" My mom gives me a horrified look.

"She's okay." Eager for a change of subject, I introduce Quinn to my mom's friends, who all give her a warm welcome.

"Join us," Gloria says, scooting over to the end of the couch she's sitting on alone.

"Andrew, get the girl a drink, will you?" Mom says.

I hesitate just a second before going to the kitchen, practically running to get there and back as fast as I can. I pour two white wines from the open bottle on the counter, though I prefer bourbon.

When I walk back into the room, it's quiet and my mom is looking at Quinn expectantly.

"From Des Moines," Quinn says. "I started school at University of Iowa but dropped out after my sophomore year to move here."

"And pursue what?" my mom asks.

I clear my throat and sit down next to Quinn, handing her one of the glasses in my hand.

"Some sort of nonprofit work, I think," Quinn says, taking a sip from the glass.

"Nonprofit work?" My mother's look of distaste is almost comical.

"So, how have you been, Mom?" I ask, resting a hand on Quinn's knee.

"I'm well, dear."

"If you'll excuse us," I say to the group, "I want to take Quinn to watch the parade from the balcony windows while it's still going. We'll be back."

She lets me help her up with a hand, and I lead the way across the apartment to the French doors that open onto a balcony. It's too cold to stand outside, but I point out the parade through the glass in the doors and Quinn smiles.

"I've never missed one in the years I've been here," she says.

"We always found a good spot to watch it."

"So you're from Iowa?"

She nods and sips the wine. "Mm-hmm."

"You don't have a Midwestern accent."

"Hmm."

Quinn turns and takes in the apartment, decorated in muted cream and rose tones. Mom has some of the vases she's collected while traveling displayed in a glass case, but her apartment is mostly designed around showcasing her art. She's a passionate collector of paintings.

"So is this where you grew up?" she asks.

"No, we had a place on the Upper East Side. Mom moved here when I was at NYU."

I can't stop looking at Quinn's legs in those dark brown tights. Behind my polite expression, I'm having dirty thoughts about how much I'd like to rip them off of her so I can feel her smooth, soft skin.

"I had to tell her something," Quinn says softly. "I figured Iowa was as good a place as any."

Her expression is somber, and I hate the shame I see there. I put my arms around her and pull her against my chest.

"I don't care what she thinks," I say, speaking gently into her ear. "You don't need to be anyone but you."

I feel her single note of laughter against my chest. "I don't even know who that is anymore."

"You're courageous. Loyal. Strong. Beautiful."

She looks up at me wistfully. "I don't belong here, in the arms of a rich man who graduated from MIT. I'm a high school dropout. I used to climb around in Dumpsters and eat garbage." Her voice is nearly a whisper, and it's filled with emotion.

"You're the most amazing woman I've ever been with," I say, brushing the hair back from her face. "Don't ever doubt yourself. You're a survivor."

"Am I? Is it really surviving if you put yourself into a stupid situation you didn't even have to be in?"

I take her hand and lead her across the apartment to a guest bedroom, closing the door behind us. There's a small loveseat in front of a fireplace, and I sit down, turning to face her as she sits down beside me.

"There's nothing stupid about you, Quinn," I say. "Where's this self-doubt coming from?"

She sighs deeply. "I miss Bethy. And I can't stop wondering if I failed her somehow. I haven't been to school since I was sixteen, but she was *eleven*, Andrew. Eleven. There's so much she missed out on. What about the rest of her life? She never even started high school."

"Why did you leave your life?"

She furrows her brow and looks away. "I thought it was for a good reason, but now I wonder if maybe I was wrong. I just didn't feel like I had any other choices. I was desperate."

I lace our fingers together and hold her gaze. "I know you're afraid to trust me, but if I knew all your truths, I'd keep them locked up forever."

Her smile goes all the way to her eyes. "You're so much more than I was expecting."

"You, too."

I put a hand on her back to pull her close, leaning in at the same time. I kiss her slow and easy at first, but soon I can't hold back. I take her hips and slide her onto my lap, my tongue brushing across hers as I pull her against me.

"Let's take a trip," I say against her neck as I kiss it. "Anywhere in the world. I'll drop everything to go. Just tell me where."

"Anywhere," she says. "I'd go anywhere with you."

I slide a hand into her hair and kiss her hard, wishing like hell we weren't at my mom's house. I want to be closer to

Quinn right now. I want to chase away all her self-doubt and sadness and just revel in how she makes me feel. So *alive*. I've never felt so alive.

"I don't care what your reasons for leaving your old life were," I say, holding her tightly against me. "None of that matters to me. Only you matter. I'll protect you from anything and everything, Quinn."

She slides her hands around my neck and kisses me, moaning softly into my mouth. I want to consume her in this moment; make every inch of her a part of me.

A sharp knock sounds at the door, and we both turn as it opens.

"*Oh*," my mom says, looking both scandalized and pissed at the same time. "What is this? You spend ten seconds with our guests and then sneak away for a groping session?"

"Ah . . . it wasn't intentional," I say.

She gives me a skeptical look.

"We'll be right back in, promise." I smile at her. "Almost done groping."

She closes the door, and I squeeze Quinn's ass, groaning softly as my erection presses against her.

"Stop, she can *hear* you," Quinn whispers frantically in my ear.

"I've made no secret of my feelings." I kiss her neck again.

She slides off my lap and walks to the mirror to fix her hair and straighten her clothes.

"You'd rather be out there than in here?" I ask, adjusting myself as I stand up.

"No, but we can pick this up later."

"We most definitely will." I approach her from behind and wrap my arms around her, cupping one of her breasts and reminding her again that I have a raging hard-on for her.

"Let's go," she says with a smile in her voice.

Mom and her friends are passing trays of hors d'oeuvres when we walk into the kitchen.

"Dinner will be done in about ten minutes," Mom says.

She always has her cook prep the side dishes in advance, and she heats them up and makes the turkey herself. I slip on oven mitts and take a dish of sweet potato casserole from her as she pulls it out of the oven.

"Dining room?" I ask.

"Yes, please."

"Let me know if I can help," Quinn offers. My mom doesn't respond.

"Mom," I say sternly.

"Hmm? Oh, I think we've got it covered," she says to Quinn.

I give my mother a pointed look and take the casserole into the dining room. Her table is about the size of a football field, and it's decked out with a cloth tablecloth and napkins, floral centerpieces, and china. Classical music is playing over the apartment's sound system.

When I walk back into the kitchen, Gloria is shaking her head and looking at Quinn.

"I don't know what it is," she says, "but you are just *so* familiar to me."

Quinn shrugs and smiles. "Maybe you've seen me around the city."

Gloria draws her brows together. "Did you ever intern at MAC?"

"No, I didn't."

"And you never went to NYU?"

Quinn shakes her head. "Just the University of Iowa."

"Have you done any work with the Center for Abducted Children? I'm on the board there."

The color drains from Quinn's cheeks. She clears her throat. "No, I sure haven't."

I go to Quinn and wrap her in my arms. I can feel the tension in her body.

"Let's go carve that bird," I say.

I rub a palm over her back and pick up the platter my mom has the golden brown turkey on. She left the knife on the table, and I set to work. Quinn leans against the wall in the dining room, still looking shaken.

"You okay?" I ask in a low tone.

She nods silently.

"You want to do some shopping tomorrow?" I ask. "Maybe get some gifts in the mail for a certain someone?"

"That would be nice," she says, smiling weakly.

"Nothing like the day after Thanksgiving in the city. I'll brave it for you."

I take a bite of turkey over and put it in her mouth. "Good?"

"It's very good."

"When you only cook one thing, you get really good at it," I say with a wry smile.

"I *heard* that," my mother says from the kitchen.

I steer the dinner conversation toward mundane topics like the economy and our city's mayor, making sure nothing comes up that would make Quinn uncomfortable. We stay for a couple hours after the meal, and then I announce we're leaving.

We say our good-byes, and I can feel Quinn relax as we step onto the penthouse elevator. I know she wants to keep her secrets, but I can't stay silent about this.

"Gloria mentioning the Center for Abducted Children gave you a scare," I say.

Her sigh is all the acknowledgement I get.

"Hey," I say softly. She turns to me. "Were you kidnapped, Quinn? Is that what you and your sister are running from?"

The horrors she may have been through are flying through my head. The anger burning through me right now is even worse than what I felt for the men who attacked her.

She shakes her head and gives me a sad smile.

"No. I wasn't the one who was kidnapped. I was the kidnapper."

Chapter Nineteen

Andrew

"THE *KIDNAPPER*? WHAT do you mean by that?"

Quinn swallows hard and looks down at the elevator floor.

"I took my sister. I took her away from our home."

Her voice is so soft I can hardly hear it, but there's no mistaking the anguish there.

The elevator doors open into the parking garage of my mom's building. A couple teenagers are standing there waiting. I take Quinn's hand and squeeze it as we walk to my Land Rover. As soon as we're both inside, I turn to her.

"Why did you take her?"

She's staring at her lap. "I was getting her out of a bad situation. Or . . . a potentially bad one. It's . . . hard to talk about."

Her voice is shaking along with her hands. I put my hand on her thigh.

"Remember what I said? You've got my support. Always, Quinn."

"Thanks."

"It's Paul, isn't it?" I say gently.

Her head snaps up, and she gives me a horrified look. "How do you know?"

"You've said his name when you're having nightmares."

Tears well in her eyes. "Why didn't you *tell* me?"

"I didn't think you wanted me to know."

She puts her hands over her face and cries softly. Now I'm the one who's horrified.

"Hey, no . . . Quinn . . . no, no, no. Please don't cry."

The cries turn into full-on sobs. I freeze for a second, wondering what to do. Should I let her cry or comfort her? The sound of her in pain proves too hard to ignore, so I reach over and pull her into my arms.

"I haven't . . . heard anyone . . . say his name . . . in so long," she says through her sobs. "Out loud. It's been so long."

"I'm sorry, beautiful. I didn't mean to upset you."

She just cries against my chest for a couple minutes, clinging to my back like her life depends on holding on. I could cry myself, seeing her hurting so badly. Quinn is so strong that I don't know how to help her when she's crumbling.

When she pulls away, her eyes are red-rimmed and swollen. She has mascara smeared on her face. I pass her a handkerchief, and she smiles.

"Thanks. I'm the death of these things, huh?"

"Who is Paul, Quinn? How did he hurt you?"

"I can't talk about that. Everything I've already told you is more than I ever wanted anyone to know."

I shift in my seat, feeling like a caged animal. "What if I could help you? Whoever he is, whatever he did, if he's after you . . . I can take care of it."

"Take care of it? What does that mean?"

"It means anyone who hurts you is at the top of my shit list. You're upset, and I want to take care of it."

She stares out the windshield at the concrete wall. "It's just not that simple, Andrew."

"It can be. When I put my mind to something, I make it happen."

"What, you mean like *killing* him?"

"If that's what it takes."

She exhales deeply. "We shouldn't even be talking about this. Can we just go home?"

"Of course." I start the car and look over my shoulder to back out of the parking spot.

I can't stop thinking about Quinn as a teenager, bringing her little sister to the streets of New York to hide from whoever this Paul guy is. It was a gutsy move. My admiration for her grows even stronger.

With my resources, I could find out who she is and who Paul is in a matter of a day. I feel a burning urge to do it—and to make sure Paul knows his life depends on never coming near Quinn or Bethy again.

I have an impossible choice to make: protect the woman I'm falling for or hold on to her trust in me. I want both of those things so fucking badly I can see them consuming me.

Quinn

I SLEPT SO soundly in Andrew's arms last night. We watched movies all afternoon and evening, and then he worked his bedroom magic on me twice—once with his mouth and another with his fingers. I felt the stress of the day melting away as I climbed high and came down both times.

This morning, the smell of cooking bacon and brewing coffee draws me into the kitchen. Andrew looks up from the stove, and I approach him with a smile, wrapping my arms around him from behind.

"You really know how to take care of a girl," I say, pressing my cheek to his firm back.

He puts down the spatula and turns, wrapping his arms around me. "Thanks for letting me take care of you. I know it's hard for someone so independent."

"It is. But it feels good."

I reach up and cup his stubbled cheek, then tip up on my toes to kiss him. He tastes like coffee.

"We're going to get the dog?" he asks when I pull away. "Or shopping first?"

"Let's shop first so we don't have to leave him here alone."

Andrew breaks off a piece of bacon from the plate next to the stove and puts it in his mouth. He scrambles some eggs and then puts them in a big bowl.

"What do you want to get Bethy for Christmas?" he asks.

"I don't know . . . maybe some caramel corn from the place we always liked the smell of. And some books."

"How about a car?"

I look up from the cup of coffee I'm pouring and accidentally overfill it. "A car? She can't even drive."

"Won't she be learning?"

"I don't know. She's not in school. Maybe Bean will teach her. But a car is . . . a lot."

"Would she like it?"

"Oh, Andrew," I laugh as I wipe up the coffee I spilled on the counter. "It's dangerous how that's your only criteria."

"Only when it comes to you. And your sister."

I'm so attached to this complex, thoughtful, sweet, sexy, controlling man. Already, I can't imagine life without him.

"Not a car," I say. "But thanks for offering."

"Cell phone. So you guys can talk."

I nod. "I would love that. But I worry about it being tracked."

"I can take care of that."

I arch a brow at him. "What *can't* you take care of?"

"Who would track it, anyway? You're safe here."

"She's not really findable right now. I guess I still am, though." I lean against the kitchen counter and sip my coffee. "When we first got here, we had a couple hundred dollars I'd saved up. It went fast. We got hungry after that, and we went to a soup kitchen. We were in line, and I looked over and saw a missing children poster with our photos on it. It scared me to death. I grabbed her, and we ran. That's why I was afraid to go to a shelter or a soup kitchen after that."

"Damn. I truly can't imagine, Quinn. What you've been through."

"I worried every single day that they'd find us and send me to jail and her back home. That was my nightmare."

"You were a minor, though. I don't know that you can even be charged with a crime."

I sigh deeply. "I don't care about that as much as I care about keeping her safe. She'll be eighteen in two years, and I have to keep her safe until then."

"I can get her a phone that's not trackable. You guys could talk every day."

Just the thought brings a lump to my throat. "If it's possible . . . I'd love that."

"Maybe a laptop, too? Would she like that?"

"I'm sure she'd love it."

My breakdown yesterday was a catharsis. I feel like I released some of the worry, and it was good to get it off my shoulders.

Andrew and I laugh a lot over breakfast, and then spend a blissful couple of hours shopping.

We buy Bethy a laptop, a necklace, an e-reader, several paperbacks, and two pairs of shoes. I help Andrew pick out some scarves and perfume to give his mother for Christmas.

After a quick lunch, we go to the animal hospital. My heart pounds as we walk through the door. I'm excited to see the sweet boy who rescued me that day in the alley.

A nurse takes us to a room and closes the door behind her.

"He was lucky to get here when he did," she says. "He was in pretty rough shape, as you know. We've had him on IV fluids and gotten him dewormed. He's got hair missing in spots on his ears that was probably eaten away by bugs. It's not likely to ever grow back. We've got his diet and meds all written down on here for you. He needs to see his regular vet in two weeks for a check. And that's about it . . . I'll go get him."

She leaves the room, and I feel like an expectant mother as I wait. I've never had a dog, but I know this dog was meant to be mine.

When the nurse walks him into the room on a leash, I start crying unexpectedly. He's still skinny, but he's clean now. He's a golden retriever, and his hair has been washed, cut, and combed. I see the spots on his ears without hair, but they don't make him any less handsome.

I kneel on the floor, and he approaches me slowly.

"Hello, sweetheart," I say in a soothing tone. "I'm your mama now."

Andrew sits down next to me and reaches for the dog's ears, but the dog moves back in fear.

"It's all right, guy," he says. "I can't believe how dirty you were. Never even knew you had that gold coat under there. You've got the Midas touch, huh?"

I smile at Andrew. "Let's call him Midas."

"Yeah?" He offers the dog his flat palm. "You do look like a Midas. King Midas Wentworth."

Midas sniffs his fingers. We spend a few minutes getting acquainted before Andrew pays the bill, and we settle into the

Land Rover with Midas on my lap.

"He's shaking," I say, running my hands over his back to soothe him.

"He'll be better when we get home."

"He's probably not house-trained."

"We'll work on it."

I feel a surge of happiness. "Thank you for letting him stay."

"He saved you, right? This dog's gonna live in luxury now."

"Hey, about the trip you mentioned yesterday . . ."

He looks over, brows arched. "You think of a place you want to go?"

"I think we should wait a couple weeks. I don't want to leave Midas right now."

"Sure, we can wait. And when we go, we can take him with us."

"I'd like that."

My worries are still there, but there's also a new sense that everything is okay. Bethy is safe. I'm as happy as I can be without her here. I write her a letter when we get back home.

Dear Bethy,

It makes me so happy to know you're settling in well there. Tell Bean it means everything to me that he's keeping you safe. I wish I was there on the beach with you. One day I will be.

Life here is good. Andrew is so much more than I was expecting. We have a dog now, his name is Midas. I know you'll love him when you meet him. I think you'll like Andrew, too. He's a little intense at times, but that's one of the things I like best about him.

I started volunteering at a homeless shelter. It feels good to be helping there. It's hard to see people who need so much and only be able to give them a meal, but it's something. Women and children get to stay at the shelter, but men can only get food there.

I got to see a bit of the Thanksgiving parade yesterday, and it reminded me of our times watching it. Lots of good memories, like doing that dance in the alley with you after the parade one year.

I'm proud of you for learning Spanish and working with a tutor. I always knew you were strong, and it feels good to see you holding your own.

Please write me as much as you can. I miss you and think of you often. We'll be together again soon.

Love,

Quinn

Chapter Twenty

Andrew

JET LAG'S A bitch. I've been dragging through the whole flight home, but now that we're about to land, I'm feeling energized again.

After Quinn and I spent an incredible Thanksgiving weekend together, I found out Monday morning that I had to make an unplanned trip to Hong Kong. It took several days of meetings to wrap up a real estate deal, so I had to stay all week.

It'll be Friday evening New York time when I land, and I can hardly wait to see Quinn. We texted a lot while I was gone, but it's not the same. I miss waking up to the citrusy smell of her hair and hearing her voice as soon as I walk in from work.

I miss her body, too. Now that I know exactly what gets her going, there's no place I'd rather be than in bed with her. She's the most responsive woman I've ever been with and it's addictive. Every moan and arch of her back give me a high.

We finally touch down, and I text her that I've landed. I'm still wearing a suit since I flew home immediately after a meeting, but I'm sure it looks less than stellar by now. I like my suits newly dry cleaned and my shirts freshly pressed, but right now that's the furthest thing from my mind. I'm only thinking about seeing Quinn and getting this suit off.

Roy's waiting for me. He drives me home with little conversation, and when I step off the elevator from the parking garage, Quinn is in the kitchen fanning something on the stove with an oven mitt.

"Fuck this," she mutters. I smile and walk toward her.

She looks up and gives me a halfhearted smile. "Hey, I was cooking you dinner."

"Yeah?"

"Hope you're not hungry. I burned it."

I toss my jacket, tie, and shoulder bag onto the island. "I'm not hungry."

"Good."

She's got her hair pulled back, and I admire the long, lean line of her neck. My gaze wanders down, taking in every inch of her in profile.

"That apron looks hot on you," I say, taking her by the hips to bring her closer.

"Yeah?"

I bring my mouth down on hers for a hungry kiss before answering. "Yeah. I missed you bad, Quinn."

"I missed you, too." She brings a hand up to stroke my bristled cheek. "No hooker action over there, right?"

I'm taken aback for a second. "Are you asking me if I fucked any hookers?"

She looks just a bit sheepish. "Yes. I don't know our rules. And you haven't had sex in . . . well, at least for the seven weeks I've been here, right?"

I can't be defensive. She's looking for reassurance, and I want to give that to her. It just floors me that she thinks I could even consider another woman, given my feelings for her.

"I haven't touched another woman since before I met you,"

I say, meeting her eyes. "Scout's honor."

"You were a Boy Scout?"

"Briefly. I wanted to earn a merit badge by studying their corporate hierarchy and suggesting ways they could become more efficient, and the brass didn't care for that idea."

She laughs; that warm, rich sound is my new favorite. "And you were how old?"

"Twelve."

With her thumb, she traces a line across my lips and over my jawline. "You were destined for greatness," she says softly.

"I think so. You're pretty great, and destiny drew us together."

Her eyes soften. "That sounds awfully romantic coming from you."

"What can I say? You make me feel romantic."

"You make me feel happy," she says with a smile. "So happy."

"I want to take you to bed and make you feel all sorts of happy." I kiss her neck, and she draws in a breath.

"Andrew, I'm ready," she says in my ear.

"Me too. Let's go."

She pulls back and meets my gaze. "No, I mean . . . *ready*."

My pulse kicks into overdrive. "Yeah?"

Her tongue darts out to moisten her pink lips. "Yeah."

A marching band bursts into action in my head. This, I wasn't expecting. I've been making a concerted effort not to pressure her into sex, and her blow jobs are epic enough to hold me over indefinitely.

"Yeah," I repeat, but it comes out of my lips laced with the deep desire I've been building for her all this time.

I take hold of her hips and pick her up. She wraps her legs around my waist. I head in the direction of my bedroom, stopping every few feet to kiss her.

Finally. I haven't just been waiting for this for the seven weeks I've known Quinn. It's been a whole lot longer. I've never wanted a woman so much I'd wait patiently. Never known one who made me forget there were other women out there. And never have I thought a woman like Quinn, so utterly perfect, would willingly give herself to me this way.

Quinn

WE'VE ALMOST MADE it to the bedroom. My heart is pounding, and I'm hot all over. I've been thinking about this moment the whole time Andrew was gone. It wasn't supposed to go down exactly like this. We were supposed to enjoy the delicious casserole I made, and then I was going to tell him over dessert that I was ready for the next step.

But this'll work, too. In fact, this is working *very well.* My whole body is humming with pent-up arousal. I'm not nervous. Not with Andrew. I'm just ready.

He stops in the doorway to the bedroom, but this time instead of kissing me, he gives me a serious look.

"I need to know this isn't about the money," he says.

"The money?"

"Yeah. We don't have to do this. I don't . . . *expect it* in exchange for the money. All I want is you."

His deep blue eyes are pleading with me to believe him. I wonder if anyone else has been allowed to see past his cool, detached, always in control façade. I like that side of him, but this side—the vulnerable, caring side, is the one I'm irrevocably attached to. Like the life experiences that brought me here, he's etched on my heart now.

"It's not about the money," I say gently. "I don't care about the money. All I want is you, too."

"I'm over our arrangement. If you want ten times or a hundred times as much as we agreed on, I'd give it to you. I want to share everything I have with you."

"I know. But everything I want from you, I already have. It's here with me right now."

His gaze wavers slightly with emotion, and then he leans closer and devours my mouth in a kiss so consuming I'm left breathless.

"I can stop at any time," he says, walking me to the bed.

"Do we need, like . . . a safe word?"

He cocks an amused brow at me, his face shadowed in the room's dim light. "A safe word?"

"It's something I've read in books," I say quickly.

"Oh. Well, I'm not into BDSM, so how about 'stop' or 'no'? Those words'll work fine."

I nod. "And if I like it, I'll say, 'Oh, God . . . *yes*. More, Andrew, *more*.' Just like that."

He steps closer to me until I'm forced to fall back onto the bed, and then he climbs on with a knee between my thighs.

"Now you're teasing me," he says in a low tone.

"Maybe."

With a groan, he dips his face to my neck, kissing me from there down to my chest. My mouth is open in silent bliss as the scruff on his face brushes over my sensitive skin, making me tingle.

I wrap my arms around his back, taking in the feel of his muscles and the faintly spicy scent of his soap. I missed everything about him when he was gone.

He peels my clothes off slowly, his expression one of reverence as his lips taste my newly exposed skin. He already knows every inch of me, but this time feels different.

I tug at his clothes, and he helps me take them off. Then we're skin-to-skin, and I feel heat between my thighs just from this closeness. He's still exploring me with his mouth and hands, and it's almost more than I can take.

Just his warm breath on my nipple makes me shiver and moan with pleasure. When he closes his lips over it, I gasp and pull his hips against me with my legs around his waist.

"You're eager," he says, his eyes locked on mine while his lips hover over my wet, hardened nipple.

"Yes," I say in a breathy tone. "Haven't we waited long enough?"

His lips curve into a smile. "Not much longer, baby."

Then he takes my hips and flips me over. He kisses his way from my shoulder blade down my back, and then farther.

"I love this ass," he says, giving it a playful smack as he kisses the spot right beneath it.

I'm a panting mess, wound so tight I think I could explode at any second. Andrew discovers that the back of my knee is a sensitive spot, and he takes extra time kissing me there. By the time he flips me back over, I'm feeling desperate.

When he climbs on top of me again, I cling to his wide shoulders and say his name softly.

"I like that," he says in my ear.

"Andrew," I repeat. "I want you so much."

He groans and kisses me beneath my ear. "I want you, too. I didn't know what it was to want someone like this before you."

He eases inside me just a bit, and I moan softly. When he goes a little farther, my next moan mingles with another groan from him.

"Damn, you feel amazing," he says, his lips just an inch from mine.

I ease my hips up, and he slides in a little more, making him groan even louder. The pressure of him opening me hurts, but his sounds of pleasure are a worthy trade.

"Don't stop," I say.

He moves his hips up but then brings them back down, filling me again. I cry out, and he slides back out.

"Is that all of it?" I ask.

His laugh is a single note. "No. But I don't have to give you all of it."

"I *want* all of it."

"Well, *I* want you to enjoy this. We'll work up to it."

I meet his gaze and open my legs as wide as they'll go. "Really, Wentworth? You're going to make me beg for it?"

His eyes narrow, and I realize what all the books I've read meant about a *hooded gaze*. And it's hot. I put my feet on the backs of his thighs and urge him forward.

He pumps his hips into me, probably trying to put me in my place. But I love it, and I cry out with pleasure as he sinks a little farther into me than before.

With a low, satisfied groan, he does it again.

"You like that?" he asks.

"Yes. More."

This time when he thrusts into me, I feel more pressure. I relax my body, and as he keeps going, it lessens.

"All . . ." he says, his voice strained. "You're taking it all."

"It's good," I say against his lips. He kisses me deeply, and every one of my nerve endings falls under his control. Every thrust, every groan, every touch seems to light me up.

I just want more and more. It feels better than I ever imagined. But after about five minutes, Andrew slows down.

"No," I say softly.

"Just give me a second," he says, sliding all the way in and then out again. He goes faster again then, and I moan his name as I feel myself climbing toward release.

After a few more minutes, he gets up on his knees, where he's able to drive into me even deeper. I'm crying out incoherently because it feels so amazing. His grunts are a mixture of pleasure and pain. I can tell he's holding himself back.

He puts his thumb on my clit and circles it. Just a few seconds and I'm falling over the edge of bliss, yelling out his name as he pounds into me. He groans low and long as he comes right behind me.

It's almost too much, what I feel when he kisses me. It's a flood of adoration and satisfied need.

"Good?" I ask as he pulls me against him.

He laughs softly. "Fucking amazing."

"For me, too."

He kisses me again and then gets up to go to the bathroom, returning with a washcloth for me. I clean myself up as he climbs back into bed beside me.

There are so many things I want to say, but I can't find the right words. Andrew settles my back to his chest and pulls the covers over us. Soon I hear him snoring softly, and I feel myself dropping into a contented sleep, worries banished until morning.

Chapter Twenty-One

Quinn

A BEARDED MAN in the food line at the shelter is looking at me with his brows drawn together.

"Hey, girl . . . you okay?" he asks.

"Hmm?" I shake myself out of the daze I was in and scoop some vegetables onto his plate. "Oh, I'm sorry. I was off in my own world."

He shakes his head, probably thinking I'm a ditz. This week, I kind of have been. I think about Andrew all the time, usually with a big, dumb smile on my face. Adding sex to our relationship has brought us closer in a way I never knew possible.

When he eases away from me every morning to get up and work out, I want to pull him back into bed. One morning, he did get back in bed with me after his shower, his body warm and his muscles firm. I wove my fingers into his wet hair as we had slow, incredibly good sex.

"You need more?" another volunteer, Jasmine, asks me. I look down at my big stainless pan and see I'm almost out of vegetables.

"Yes."

She calls out to another volunteer and asks me to serve the rolls and butter while she runs to the bathroom. I take over, keeping an eye out for anyone who comes in without a coat, hat, or decent shoes. Andrew's always encouraging me to go shopping, and I've found I actually do enjoy it when I'm shopping for others.

We finish and I take a mother's energetic toddler off her hands for an hour so she can fill out job applications. I take the boy to the shelter's playroom, where we chase each other and build block towers.

When my shift at the shelter is over, Roy picks Micah and me up and drives me to the library. I volunteer at the shelter every weekday so I never have time to walk to the library, but some weekend I'm going to walk there again, just so I don't let the attack keep hold of me. I'll have to slip past my security guard shadow, Micah, but I can handle that.

Anna gives me a letter from Bethy, and I rush to the library bathroom to read it while Roy waits in the car. Micah is probably watching me right now, but he can't come into the bathroom.

I open it inside a stall, missing my sister as soon as I see her neat, cursive handwriting.

Dear Quinn,

I got the Christmas presents and put them under the tinsel tree Maria helped me make. It's a tiny, sad-looking tree, but I like it. Thank you for whatever is inside the boxes.

It makes me so happy that you're doing well. I daydream about you and Andrew. He looks like Prince Charming in my dreams. Okay, there's also some Channing Tatum in there.

I'm doing great with Spanish. I can order all our food at the market and pay for it now. Maria helps me with the other subjects, too, but it seems like we stay pretty busy taking care of her two-year-old and doing the cooking, cleaning, and laundry for me and Bean. I like having stuff to do, though. Her little girl is sweet, and I love playing with her.

Bean seems different lately. He's kind of mad sometimes, but he tries not to show it. He's just quiet a lot. He goes to a bar and drinks after work most nights. I wasn't sure if I should tell you because I don't want you to worry about me. I promise I'm fine.

I miss you so much. If you and Prince Charming decide to take a vacation, please come to Mexico so I can see you. I'm counting the days until this six months is over.

Love,

Bethy

Tears burn my eyes as I read the letter a second time. Damn it. I'm wondering once again if I've done right by my sister. We're not on the edge of survival anymore. Andrew told me I can have more money if I need it. So if she needs me and money isn't an issue, why am I still here?

For Andrew. I'm in New York falling in love with a man while Bethy is lonely in a strange country with Bean, who's started drinking. I feel like an asshole.

I put the letter in my purse and return to the car. Roy takes me to the salon I have an appointment at to get my hair and makeup done for the fundraiser Andrew and I are attending tonight.

I'm thinking about Bethy as my hair is smoothed and swept into a glamorous, pinned-up style. As my dark, smoky eye makeup is applied, I'm picturing her cooking and cleaning for a man who comes home drunk. It's all I can do not to cry.

When I get back to the warehouse and step into the fitted cream gown I'm wearing tonight, I look at my reflection in the mirror and realize Bethy's analogy was right on. I'm living like Cinderella at the ball right now. But I could and should be with her.

The hair and makeup took a long time, and I'm running late. I see Andrew glancing at his wristwatch when I walk out of the bedroom.

"Sorry," I say as I cross the living room "We can get going now."

His expression changes as he looks me over. The warmth and happiness I see there make me feel amazing and guilty at the same time.

"You look incredible," he says.

"Thank you."

He looks pretty good himself in his tux, which fits perfectly across his broad chest and shoulders. His hair is starting to curl slightly at the ends, which makes him look younger than twenty-eight.

Once he's helped me into my coat, he puts his on and we take the elevator to the garage, where Roy is waiting. Andrew holds my hand as we ride in silence.

"You have a good day?" he asks after a few minutes.

"Yes, you?"

"Not bad."

I feel him looking at my face in the dim light of the car. "Everything okay?"

I nod, because it feels like less of a lie than words would. Andrew doesn't prod, and I'm lost in my own thoughts the rest of the ride to the posh hotel. When we arrive, Andrew exits the car at the curb, and I slide out after him. He takes my hand again.

Turning my face to his shoulder, I whisper, "Everything's not okay."

"I can tell." He tips my chin up with his thumb. "What's wrong, beautiful?"

"Bethy."

He furrows his brow and kisses my forehead. We start the

walk inside, his arm wrapped protectively around my waist, when I look over at the flashing cameras. My stomach churns nervously.

"Shit. Andrew," I say softly.

"Oh, hell." He turns me closer to him so my face is shielded and rushes me inside.

"Fuck," I say angrily when we're past the line of photographers. "I wasn't thinking."

"No, *I* wasn't thinking." He takes out his phone and starts typing. "I'll take care of this. Steve and his guys will come here and take care of this, okay?"

"How? Did you see all those cameras?"

"I'll buy them."

I feel a ray of hope. "You can do that?"

"I'll put Steve on it, okay? Don't worry. Let's find someplace private so we can talk."

"Not here. I'm too worried about people standing around corners."

"Okay," he says, glancing at the hotel's long, dark reception desk. "So we'll get a room."

"A room? Now?" I look from side to side to make sure no one's within earshot. "People will think we're going up there to screw."

Andrew arches his brows. "Not a man in this place will blame me when they see you."

I laugh, easing some of my built-up tension. "Flattery really will get you nowhere right now."

"I get it. The room's just to talk." He releases my hand. "Be right back."

How much do I want to tell him? While I watch him stride up to the front desk and see the woman working there blush at him like a schoolgirl, I realize Andrew doesn't know where Bethy is or why I'm hiding her. He doesn't know much about

Bean, either. I trust Andrew with my life. But can I trust him with Bethy's? If she's not safe, there's no happiness anywhere for me, with anyone. Not even Andrew.

"Miss Jones," a sharp female voice says beside me.

I look over and see Gina, Andrew's mother. *Fuck.* I am so not in the mood. She's dressed to the nines in a navy gown, her silver hair framing her elegant face.

"It's Quinn."

"I see you still have my son's eye."

"Apparently so."

"And what is he doing at the hotel desk? Is he getting a room?"

I just sigh, hoping she'll catch on to my annoyance and leave.

"Oh, that's *rich*," she says sarcastically. "I knew this thing between you had to be all about sex, but—"

"Fuck off," I say, meeting her icy blue gaze.

"Excuse me?"

"There's no excuse. You're a rude bitch."

Her face contorts into an expression of disbelief. "Wow. You must really think you've got a hold on him, to speak that way to his *mother*."

"Treat me like shit, and I'll treat you like shit right back."

"You've got quite a mouth on you, hmm?"

"Nastiness comes in many forms, Mrs. Wentworth."

I look over at Andrew. He's leaving the front desk and looking right at us.

"Listen here, you gold-digging whore," Gina says through clenched teeth. "My son is all I have. You may be able to manipulate him, but I see right through you."

"Mother," Andrew says sharply, "what's going on here?"

"Just chatting with Quinn," she says with a smile.

"Uh, no. I'm not covering for you." I reach for Andrew's

hand, squeezing it for strength. "She was just calling me a gold-digging whore."

"That's *bullshit,*" Andrew says to her in a low tone. "You don't even know her."

Gina raises her chin. "This isn't the time or place for this conversation."

"There won't be any more conversations between you and me until you've apologized to Quinn and you treat her appropriately."

Andrew turns and leads me away before Gina can get another word out.

"I'm sorry," he says to me as we cross the hotel's marble-floored lobby.

"It's not your fault."

"I'm still sorry. I won't allow her to overstep again."

I squeeze his hand. "Did you get a room?"

"I did."

I sigh softly as we stop at the elevator, and Andrew pushes the button. The doors slide open, we step on, and as soon as they close, I turn to him.

"I wasn't very nice to her, either. I told her to fuck off."

His lips curve up in an amused smile. "Did you now? I don't see that happening unless she asked for it."

"Yeah, she did."

"I know she can be . . . intense. She ran into me when I was out at dinner with a woman in college, and that's the only other time she's seen me with someone. Since I introduced you to her, she thinks we're serious."

"Seriously crazy, maybe," I say softly.

The elevator doors open onto the fourteenth floor, and Andrew leads the way down the hall to our room.

It's a small room with a king-size bed. We walk in, and I give Andrew a dirty look.

"What is this? It's not even a suite. Are we peasants?"

He's taken aback for a second before I let out a nervous laugh.

"Sorry," I say. "Just a bad joke. You did not have to pay for this room just so we could talk."

He shrugs. "I only got it for an hour. I told the hotel staffer you want a nice ass-fucking before the fundraiser starts, and an hour's good for that."

My mouth drops open in shock. "You . . . *what*?"

"That was my bad joke, so now we're even." He winks and sits down on the bed. "Now come here and tell me what's on your mind."

I sit down, my shoulders slumping forward. "I got a letter from Bethy. I don't like some of the things she told me."

"Can you tell me about it?"

I hesitate for a second. I trust Andrew. He's proven to me many times that he's on my side. And I really, truly *want* to talk to him about this.

"She's with Bean," I say softly. "In . . . Mexico. They have a place, and he has a job. She's getting tutored by someone there. But she said Bean's been going to a bar after work to drink. And she's cooking and cleaning and helping take care of the tutor's kid . . . while I'm *here*."

I gesture at the extravagant gown I'm wearing.

"You feel guilty," he says.

I nod. "Very. I took her away so I could take care of her, and I'm not. I've left her pretty much alone in a foreign country."

"So why don't we bring her here?"

"Back to New York?"

"Yeah. The warehouse is plenty big. She can live with us and get back in school."

I consider it for a few seconds. "I'd love that, but I'm still afraid of her being recognized. I can't let that happen."

"I can help with identification for her, too."

With a deep sigh, I decide it's time to tell him what I really want. "I want to go there. I want to see where she's at and figure out what's happening with Bean. I want to spend some time alone with her."

Andrew's expression is grim. "I understand . . . yeah. I'll help however I can."

"I don't know what will happen when I get there. If things are okay, I can come back here."

"Yeah." He doesn't look or sound like he believes that will happen.

"It's not that I don't want to be with you," I say, putting my palm on his thigh. "I do. But I have a responsibility to my sister. I'm the one who took her away, and I need to take care of her."

He nods. "It's okay, Quinn. I understand."

"I wish I could have both of you," I say, my throat tightening with emotion.

"Whomever you're up against, I can handle them. You haven't seen my darker side, but I've got one. I'm not afraid to fight for someone . . . for you."

His blue eyes are warm and full of devotion. My heart opens a little further to him.

"She'd be sent back home," I say. "I guess it's technically . . . the judicial system I'm up against."

"Who has legal custody of her?"

"Our mother."

His gaze stays locked on mine. "So we offer her money, then. It's a powerful motivator."

"Not for her."

"You mean she wouldn't want it, or she's already got it?"

"Already got it."

He nods and leans his elbows on his knees. "Damn. There's

got to be a way."

"I just need to see her so we can talk things over. Maybe if I could get her here, she'd be okay with a tutor coming to the warehouse. I hate to make her live like a shut-in, but at least we'd be together then."

"Just let me know when," Andrew says, still looking down at the floor. "I'll charter a flight for you."

"No. No flights. I'm too paranoid about someone finding out. I mean, there could be someone following me right now without me even knowing, just waiting for me to lead the way to her."

He looks over at me. "I can help with that."

I smile at his serious expression. "My grandma used to tell my grandpa that he was a dear. That's what you are to me, Andrew. My dear man who is always ready to rescue me."

"Always."

"But I need to do this on my own. Please trust me enough to let me do that."

After several beats of silence, he says, "Okay."

He kisses me softly then, and I can see the warring emotions on his face. He wants to support me, but he's disappointed. I take his face in my hands and kiss him, trying to tell him without words how much he means to me.

"I guess we should go down," he says, then clears his throat.

I just nod, not trusting myself to speak. I'm a mess of emotions right now.

We both put on a good face for the fundraiser guests. Andrew introduces me to everyone we talk to as his girlfriend, which is bittersweet. He places the winning bid on a doggie spa package for Midas at the fundraiser, and I realize yet again how hard it will be to leave.

I have to, though.

Once home, Andrew ravages me with the fiercest, most passionate sex we've had yet. He makes me come three times, and I try to commit every second to memory because soon, memories may be all I have of him.

Chapter Twenty-Two

Andrew

MIDAS SHIES AWAY when I approach him with the leash. I have to corner him and get down on my knees to get it on him.

"Hey, man, it's me," I say in a soothing tone. "I'm the guy who brought you those doggie cookies you like so much."

I pet him for a minute, and he stops shaking.

"Ready," Quinn says, walking into the kitchen wearing a white parka and a red stocking cap with a fuzzy ball on top.

She dresses warmly for our nightly walk with Midas. But I do wonder why I haven't seen any coats besides the white one.

"Hey, is that the only coat you've got?" I ask as we walk to the front door.

She looks down at it. "Yeah, other than the dress ones. Why?"

I shrug. "I just saw the charges on the account from that store you like and figured you were buying a bunch. Not that I care. You *should* buy a bunch."

"Oh. Well, I kind of did buy a bunch, but they were for people at the shelter."

Her sheepish expression makes me furrow my brow. "You didn't think I'd mind, did you?"

"I don't know . . . I should have known you wouldn't."

"Do what makes you happy. Just let me know if it costs six figures or more." I remember then that she's leaving tomorrow. "I mean . . . if you come back."

"I'll be back," she says, but I know neither of us is convinced.

I know she wants to come back—I can see it in her eyes and hear it in her voice. But not knowing what she'll find in Mexico, I know there's no way she can be sure she will. If Bethy's in a bad situation, I know Quinn will put her first. I admire that, though if it happens, I'll never be the same.

My business will thrive if she doesn't come back. Feeling empty and angry fuels my need to crush the competition and make money. I like to work day and night when I've got nothing to go home to. Which, before Quinn, was always.

We walk in silence for a couple minutes, stopping so Midas can sniff a tree. He decides it's a good place for a piss so we wait.

I'm having an inner struggle. Should I go all in with Quinn, put all my cards on the table before she leaves? It's not like it'll make her stay. She has to go take care of things with her sister. But I know if I don't tell her everything and she never comes back, I'll always wonder if I should have shown her all of me.

Midas is ready to move on so we continue down the block. A couple college-aged guys in leather coats are approaching us walking in the other direction, and I see them checking Quinn out.

They remind me too much of those assholes who beat her up. When they're about to pass us and one of them is still looking at her, I say, "You guys need something?"

They look over at me and then exchange glances.

"No, man," one of them says.

"Sorry," the other one mutters.

They keep walking. Quinn takes my free arm, and we continue, too.

"I'm going to miss you," she says, resting her head on my shoulder.

"You, too. Will you please reconsider taking your phone?"

She moves her head from my shoulder. "I'm just too worried about being tracked."

"By whom?"

"By *someone*."

"Your phone is on my account, and *no one* is accessing it. What if you run into trouble?"

She shrugs. "I've run into trouble before. I have your number, you know. I'll call from another phone if I need you."

"You're not worried someone will track that?" I ask with sarcasm.

"Well, a little . . ."

"Jesus, Quinn. You've watched too much *Law & Order*."

"Look, better safe than sorry, all right?"

I stare at the city lights in the distance. "I could find you if I wanted to. Whether you take the phone or not. You could walk away from me right now with nothing but the clothes on your back, and I could find you. But I won't. If I see you again, it has to be because you came back to me."

She stops walking and looks over at me. "How? How could you find me?"

"It doesn't matter."

"It matters a hell of a lot, Andrew, because if you could find me, so could *he*."

I step closer to her. "Tell me who he is. I'll put someone on him, and we'll know where he is all the time."

She's quiet for a few seconds, and then she finally says, "I don't want you to know. When Bethy and I came here, we started fresh. No baggage. I became a badass who'd do anything to survive and protect her. That's the woman you met. The woman you know."

"You're *all of it*, Quinn. Even the shit that made you into a badass. And I love that woman. I love you so deep and so hard that I don't know how I'll survive you leaving."

I didn't mean to let it out, but there it is. She seems to be holding her breath as she looks at me. "You . . . do? Love me. I mean, do you?"

She can barely get the words out, and tears are welling in her eyes. I wrap my hands around her upper arms and say it again.

"Yes. I love you, and with that comes a need to protect you. No one will hurt you ever again if you'll just let me all the way in."

"I love you too, Andrew." She blinks and tears drop onto her cheeks. "And we'll be together again. One way or another."

Nothing's ever been harder for me than nodding at this moment. I want to rage and yell and beat the shit out of a punching bag until I'm exhausted. But I won't spend our last night together that way. Tonight is for showing her I'm a man worth coming back to. If that's going to happen, I have to find a way to let her go.

Quinn

WE GET HOME from our walk, and Midas settles into the doggie bed Andrew put in the living room for him, content to chew on his bone.

There's something unspoken happening between Andrew and me. I can tell he's tense. I wonder if he's also hurt. He said he loves me, and I'm still leaving without my phone or any way for him to reach me. I need to make him understand that it's about me, not him.

"So what now?" I say, approaching him in the living room.

He says nothing but wraps his arms around me, pulling me in for a kiss that makes me tingle from scalp to toes. It's demanding and hungry. I feel him asking me to give him everything tonight, and that's all I want.

I return his passion, and soon my nails are sinking into the back of his neck as we kiss like it's our last night on Earth. He kicks off his shoes and picks me up, carrying me into the bedroom.

Tonight's different. I don't want to be teased until he's worked me into a frenzy. I'm already there. We pull each other's clothes off with urgency, and Andrew ends up ripping off my bra and shredding my panties in his desperation.

He pushes me onto the bed, and just as my back hits the mattress, he's inside me. He's thrusting hard and deep, grunting and biting down on my nipple as he plows into me.

"Oh . . . God," I cry. "Andrew . . ."

His mouth meets mine in a crushing kiss. My orgasm is building fast. I'm going to come hard, and just before it becomes inescapable, he stops and flips me over.

Oh . . . *fuck*. He's got me on all fours now, and he's buried so deep inside me I'm yelling his name in a pleading tone. Am I asking for mercy or more? I don't even know.

He never lets up, holding my hips as he rocks into me with savage force. This is his anger at me. It's his frustration and disappointment that I'm leaving. It's his love.

I feel it, too. I don't want to go, but I have to.

"Fuck," he says, the word coming out a primal grunt.

He flips me over again and puts my ankles on his shoulders, then starts back up with the same brute force as before. Sweat glistens on his brow and chest as he thrusts again and again, never letting up.

"Andrew," I say, taking his hand and putting his palm on my cheek, "I love you. No matter what, I love you."

His expression twists with restrained emotion. As much as I love the way he's fucking me with abandon, I can't hold on anymore. I give in and let myself come. As soon as I do, his grunt becomes a groan, and he holds himself buried inside me as he comes with a shudder.

I wrap my arms around him and pull him down onto me.

"Shit," he says, breathing heavily, "I'm sorry."

"Don't say that. Just tell me again that you love me."

He leans up so his face is right over mine. "I love you, Quinn. Come back to me. I'll protect you and Bethy from anyone who tries to hurt you."

He kisses me so softly, and sweet tears are burning my eyes when he pulls away.

He gets up to go to the bathroom, and I go right after him. When I get back to bed, he's sitting on the edge, still naked, his elbows resting on his knees.

"You okay?" I ask, climbing across the bed to hug him from behind.

"There's something I need to tell you."

I slide out from behind him, and he reaches over to switch on the bedside lamp.

"Is this an under or over the covers kind of thing?" I ask.

"Over, unfortunately."

He picks up his boxer briefs from the floor and pulls them on. I sit in bed and pull the covers up to my chest.

Andrew exhales deeply, hands on his hips, then sits down on the end of the bed so we're facing each other.

"I told you my dad died in 9/11," he says.

"Yes."

"You might say I never got over it."

"I don't think anyone should expect you to."

"No, I mean . . ." He pauses. "Okay, so after Dad died and it was me and Mom, I had a lot of anger built up. I channeled it into schoolwork, sports, and learning about computers. Computers started as a hobby but became almost an obsession by the time I was in high school. By then, I was already thinking about the possibilities. I went to MIT *and* NYU because I needed both computer science and business. Couldn't fund the computer projects I wanted to do without being successful in business to make the money for it."

"What stuff?"

"What I'm about to tell you, very few people know. Very, very few. I've signed a contract agreeing to only tell my spouse if I get married and no one else. But I need you to know."

His expression is serious. I nod my understanding.

"Four years ago, I joined with five other partners to start . . . an enterprise. We all provide an equal financial buy-in. The work we do, it's all based up on the second floor of the warehouse. And what we do is . . ." He clears his throat. "Well, it's several things, actually. It begins with hacking of terrorist communications."

"Terrorists?" I can't hide my surprise.

"Yes. We monitor their communications and pretty much lay in wait until we're ready with an op, and then we intercept communications, pretending to be the terrorists they're communicating with. We set up a meet and then infiltrate it."

"Infiltrate, meaning . . . ?"

"Whatever is the most damage we can do. We blow up supplies and command locations, take out key people, expose their operations to their enemies."

I swallow hard, trying to take it all in. My buttoned-up businessman, blowing up terrorists? I can't even process it at first.

"When you say 'we,' are you actually there doing the

blowing up? Is that where you were when you said you were in Hong Kong?"

He shakes his head. "No, I was in Hong Kong. I'm almost always doing my actual work. I've been on operations before, but it's not a good idea as a rule of thumb. Mostly we use ex-military guys for them, and they're better suited."

I take a deep breath. "So, they're upstairs? Right now?"

"Right now. This is how I got your purse back. I wrote a facial scanning program that's like nothing on the market, but it was for the guys upstairs. I'd never share that technology with the private or public sector. It's how we can keep eyes on so many of those assfucks at once. I had them track the number on the debit card I gave you and then hack into the places those guys who attacked you used it. I went to one of their houses and . . . you know."

"You hurt them, I hope?"

"Hell yeah, I hurt 'em. One of 'em punched me back, though. I broke his nose for it."

I cringe. "I can't believe I accused you of setting it up."

"Hey, we're past all that. I didn't want to put you in danger by telling you. But I felt like I needed you to know everything about me before you leave. And also that I can protect you from whatever danger you're facing, Quinn. I have resources in the highest levels of government, as well as private sector ones who don't have to adhere to any rules."

"This is a lot to take in," I say.

"I know. But I don't want you to leave here with questions about me. This is why I have so much security. The guys upstairs are in as much danger as those of us who fund them. I have to provide a completely secure place for them."

"Makes sense."

"No one will track any calls coming in or out of this place, *ever*. I have cloaking software that beats anything law enforcement has access to. Please take your phone, even if you leave it turned off."

"I will." I nod. "And this is how you got my Susanna paperwork?"

"Yes. I can get a new identity for Bethy, too. We can all start over together if you want. Leave this place behind, even. Maybe move to Paris or London. I can start a business there."

My heart is pounding hopefully. "You mean that?"

"Of course, I do. You're my everything, Quinn. Even though it's only been a couple months, I know."

"I know, too," I say, my voice breaking.

He exhales deeply. "I just needed you to know everything. We only take out the worst of the worst. People like the ones who killed my father."

"I don't judge that. I actually admire it. I learned firsthand that there are evil people in the world."

His brow is still creased with worry. "There's one more thing I want you to know."

"What?"

"I didn't used to be a guy who paid for sex. Just the idea of it turned me off. But about a year ago a woman I'd slept with said she was pregnant with my child."

I feel a deep, sick churning in my stomach. "Oh, God. You have a baby?"

"No." He says it emphatically, his eyes wide. "I made her get a paternity test after she delivered the baby. It wasn't mine. But after that I took control and only slept with women I could force to be on birth control. So that's . . ."

I give him a wry smile. "The story we can one day tell our grandkids about how we met."

He laughs and shakes his head, then turns serious again. "I put an envelope of cash in your purse. If you run into any problems, I mean *anything at all*, you call me."

"I will."

He switches off the light beside the bed and climbs in beside me. When he pulls me to him, I breathe in his scent and know for sure we'll be together again. Just the thought of the nights ahead without him tear at my heart. I could never let him go forever.

When I wake up in the morning, Andrew is sitting on the edge of the bed, already dressed for work in a dark suit. I slept through him getting up for his workout and showering.

"Roy will take you as far as you want him to," he says, not looking at me. "You should let him take you all the way."

"I can't do that," I say softly. "If it were just me, I would, but I don't take chances with my sister."

He nods, his elbows resting on his knees. "I'd take you as far as you want to go, but . . . I just can't."

I move toward him and wrap my arms around him from behind. "Stay here, okay? I'll be right back."

I can't say good-bye to him while I'm naked. I go to the bathroom and brush my teeth, then to the closet where I dress in jeans and an NYU sweatshirt.

Andrew's standing by the bed when I return. I go to him, and he pulls me into his arms, neither of us saying a word for a full minute.

When I speak, it's hard to get past the lump in my throat. "No matter what happens, please know . . . I want to come back. I want to be with you."

He tightens his hold on me, and we stay like that for another minute. When he pulls away, he still won't look at me.

"Call me," he says. "I love you."

And with that, he leaves the room. I miss him already.

Chapter Twenty-Three

Quinn

I'VE BEEN TRAVELING for three full days. Considering it's been more than four years since I've driven a car, I think I've done pretty well.

Roy drove me out of the city, and then I hitched a ride out of New York State with a truck driver. I found a sedan at a Pennsylvania used car lot with a price of $2,000 painted on the windshield and paid the owner of the lot $3,000 to let me take it without any paperwork. He gave me a set of valid plates but told me he'd report the car stolen in a month if I don't bring it back by then.

Then I drove for two long days to get to the border. I stopped at a motel to sleep for a night and I wanted to call Andrew so much it hurt, but I didn't. I brought my phone but plan to leave the power off. Worrying that his phone might be tapped is irrational, but I've had to be a little irrational to make it this far since leaving home.

I use the Susanna Hopkins paperwork Andrew gave me to cross the border, holding my breath the entire time. So many things could go wrong. If I get caught, I'll be giving away

Bethy's location.

But the guards seem unfazed as they approve my passage. I don't breathe easy until I'm another few miles down the road, though. I'd like to keep going now that I'm in the same country as Bethy, but it's the end of the second day, and after fifteen hours of driving, I'm beat.

I'm able to get a room for the night with American money, and I crash as soon my head hits the pillow. The next day I set off early, exchanging some of the cash Andrew gave me for pesos. Without the $10,000 he gave me, this trip would have been near impossible. I've already sent Bean the other money I had.

Barra de Potosi is reachable in one long day of driving. I have to navigate with paper maps, which isn't easy.

Finally, I reach the sleepy town, but then I can't find the apartment. I have to stop several times and show people the paper I have the address written on. They try to give me directions, but the language barrier makes it hard for me to figure out what they're saying.

It takes me nearly an hour, but I finally think I've found the place when the sun is starting to set. The teenage boy who led me here assured me it was the right spot, and I gave him a handful of money.

I knock on the door, my heart pounding anxiously. When Bethy opens it and sees me, she bursts into tears.

"Quinn!" She throws herself at me and holds on as tight as Andrew did the morning I left.

I hug her back, squeezing my eyes closed to fight back the tears.

"How are you here?" she asks incredulously.

"I drove."

"From New York?"

"Yes."

She steps aside and pulls me in by the arm. "You must be

exhausted. Get in here."

I'm taken aback when I step inside the cramped apartment. Cramped is too generous a word for it. The living room and kitchen area are less than a hundred square feet total. The closets in Andrew's warehouse are bigger than this place.

There's a threadbare couch, and the walls are empty. It's clean but depressing.

"I know it's not much," Bethy says, tucking her hair behind her ear self-consciously.

"How are you?" I turn to her and take both her hands in mine. "I mean, how are you, really? I read between the lines of your last letter, and I'm worried."

Tears glisten in her eyes. "I'm great. Everything here is good."

"Don't lie to me. We don't lie to each other, Bethy."

She blinks and tears slide down her cheeks. "It's . . . kind of awful. I'm lonely. But I'm okay. I'm okay, Quinn. I know you want me to be here where I'm safe, and I understand that."

"No. I don't want you unhappy. We have other options now."

"We do?" Her expression lights up hopefully.

I nod. "I'm getting you out of here."

She throws her arms around me and cries some more.

"I'm so glad to see you," she says softly.

"Me too. I've missed you so much."

When she pulls away, she wipes her cheeks with her fingertips and walks a few feet to the stove.

"How about some soup?" she asks. "It's probably not the best soup ever, but it's decent."

"I'd love some."

She dips a coffee cup into the kettle and fills a bowl for me.

"So is Maria gone for the day?" I ask.

"She stopped coming about ten days ago."

"Why? I thought she was tutoring you."

Bethy shrugs. "She was, but Bean stopped paying her. She had to get another job."

I close my eyes for a few seconds. I am *pissed*. Bean had more than enough money to work with, and he's clearly not using it to take care of Bethy.

The soup is water, spices, and chunks of fish. It's awful, but I eat it because Bethy ate some before I got here. This is what she's been living like while I've been having delicious food prepared by Turner every night. Andrew's fridge is always stocked with fresh produce, yogurt, cheese, and other snacks. Bethy's fridge is pretty much empty, and it doesn't even keep what little is inside it cold.

"I want to see your room," I tell her.

I see a slight cringe as she leads the way. It hardly has enough space for the bare mattress on the floor, and there's a cord strung between two walls with Bethy's clothes hanging from it.

"At least I'm warm," she says. "And safe."

I just nod. Inside, I'm fuming. Twenty thousand dollars and this is how they're living. I wonder where the money's actually going.

"Let's go walk on the beach," Bethy says.

"When will Bean be back?"

"Usually, he doesn't get here for another couple hours."

It's only a couple blocks to the soft white sandy beach. Even though the sun is down, I can tell this is a beautiful place. The sound of lapping water and the salty smell in the air make me feel rejuvenated. I'm so glad I listened to my gut and came here.

"Tell me about Andrew," Bethy says as we walk arm in arm.

I smile. "He's a hard man to know, but now that I've gotten closer to him . . . I'm in love."

She squeezes my arm with excitement. "Really? Oh, Quinn.

You deserve it."

"He's very protective. So handsome. Supersmart. A little impatient. Generous. Sweet."

"I'm swooning here."

I bump my shoulder against hers playfully. "This is what I get for raising you on romance novels."

"He sounds like Mr. Darcy."

Her statement makes me laugh. "You know, there is some resemblance."

"Did you allow him to tell you how ardently he admires you?"

"Oh, most definitely. He wanted to come here with me, actually."

"Why didn't you bring him?"

I look out at the dark ocean waves. "I just wanted to do this myself. I still worry about us being found."

"I know. Me too."

"Do you miss home?"

She says nothing for a few seconds. "I miss some things, but I think we were right to leave."

"Do you really? Do you feel that in your heart?"

"I do. We both know what would have happened if we'd stayed."

I stop and sit down on the beach, taking off my shoes and squishing my toes into the sand. Bethy sits down beside me.

"You know," I say, "I used to keep things from you to protect you. When we were in New York. It was never anything big, really. I just never let on how scared I really was. But I think it's time we agree that we'll share everything with each other. Even the scary, ugly stuff."

"I promise."

"Me too." We sit in silence for a few seconds. "Andrew's willing to take us to another country to live. I imagine he'd need some time to get his business stuff in order, but . . . it's an idea."

"I'd love that," Bethy says softly. "I'd live with you guys?"

"Yes. I think you and I will go to another country from here, and then I'll contact him. It's best if no one knows where we are or where we're going."

"What about Bean?"

"He's not coming."

She sighs softly. "I think we should go get our stuff and leave before he gets back. He'll be mad if we tell him."

"Okay, let's go."

We dust the sand off our clothes and head back. Much as I'd like to confront Bean about the money, I know Bethy is right. What really matters is getting her out of here safely.

When we walk back into the apartment, though, Bean is there. As soon as he sees me, his expression morphs into disbelief.

"Quinn?" He grins and jumps up from the rickety kitchen table he's eating at. "You came back."

He embraces me, and I immediately smell alcohol on him.

"You've been drinking," I say flatly.

He steps back, his brow furrowed. "Yeah, I have a drink at the end of a long workday. What's it matter?"

I feel Bethy tensing beside me. *We just need to go*, I remind myself. The money doesn't matter.

"Bean, I can't thank you enough for taking care of Bethy. I just missed her too much, so I came here to get her."

He narrows his eyes. "You're leaving?"

"Things are going well for me in New York. I'm staying there."

Bean lunges toward me, forcing me to step back.

"You still want to be that rich guy's *whore*? What the hell is wrong with you? I've been here waiting and taking care of Bethy, and now you're just gonna ditch out?"

"I'm sure you've still got some of the money left," I say. "Keep it."

He shakes his head and stalks closer to me, forcing me against the wall. "No fucking way. $60K. That was the deal."

"No, it wasn't."

He punches the wall right next to my head, and I hear pieces of it crumble to the floor.

"You want to fuck me over after all we've been through and take her with you?" he yells in my face. "Not without my other forty grand."

I wrap my hand around the blade of my knife and he sneers at me, then shoves my wrist against the wall. He presses his arm with no hand against my chest to keep me in place.

"I *know* you," he says in a low, ominous tone. "I taught you to use this blade, remember?"

"I remember you saying you'd take care of Bethy, too, and look at this place. Where's the money really going, Bean?"

His expression darkens. "None of your fuckin' business."

"My sister was nothing more than a meal ticket to you. You're a disgusting pig."

He knees me in the stomach then, and I double over in pain.

"She's safe, isn't she?" He bends down to yell in my face. "Huh?"

I look up just in time to see Bethy raise something in the air and bring it down on his head with all her strength. He stumbles and falls to the floor but stays conscious. I climb on top of his back to restrain him.

"Ties," I say frantically. "We need something to tie him with."

"You bitch," Bean mutters. "I'm gonna knock your ass out."

Bethy races into her bedroom, and I twist Bean's arms around his back until he howls.

"Move and I'll break one," I say in a steady tone. "Seriously, do it. I want to break one of your arms so bad right now."

He twitches, and I twist a little harder. He groans through gritted teeth. Sweat drips from his brow to the stained tile floor.

Bethy returns with the clothesline.

"Perfect," I say.

I hold Bean in place, and she wraps the cord around his torso and arms. After it's wrapped around him several times, I pull it tight, making him wince. We tear several T-shirts into strips, and I use them to tie the cords at his back around a leg of the kitchen table. I wrap a few around his mouth as a gag so he can't scream as soon as we walk out and attract help from neighbors.

There's a murderous gleam in Bean's eyes as he watches me. I'm so angry about what he did that I'd like to stab him and let him bleed out right here, alone. But I can't forget the good he did for us in New York.

Bethy gathers the gifts under the makeshift Christmas tree and waits wide-eyed by the door.

I bend down and look into Bean's eyes. "You'll never see us again. And if you try, I'll kill you."

He chuckles through the gag. I draw my knife and rest the tip of the silver blade against his throat. He goes still.

"You come close to my sister ever again, and I will kill you, Bean."

His silence is all the acknowledgment I'll get.

"Got my keys?" I ask Bethy.

"Yes. And your purse."

I walk backward to the door, my knife still drawn.

"Have a nice life, Bean," I say as I close the door.

I hear him struggling to break free as Bethy and I bolt for the car. I start it and drive away, leaving a cloud of dust behind us.

"Oh my God," Bethy says. "I can't believe that just happened."

I take a deep breath. "I know."

"I'm scared, Quinn. He has connections down here to a lot of bad people. I think it's a cartel."

"What the hell?" I turn to her. "Why were you keeping this from me? Do you know what might have happened to you?"

"I was trying to be strong," she says defensively. "I knew you could get through it, so I told myself I could, too."

I take a few more breaths. "Okay. Okay, so let's think. He'll be able to get untied, and then what? Will he know which way we went?"

"I don't know. How could he?"

"Fuck." I slam my hand against the steering wheel. "The car has Pennsylvania plates. We're like sitting ducks in this thing if he has connections. We have to get rid of it."

I try to scan the scenery around us, but it's too dark to see much. We're on a dirt road, and there's a small café nearby.

This isn't like New York, where there are so many people we can easily hide in plain sight. And if Bean finds us, I have no doubt he'll hurt me. The rage in his eyes was unmistakable.

I park at the café, and we get out of the car. My hands are shaking as I take my purse and small travel bag from the car and dig through them in search of my phone.

It's buried at the bottom of my purse, still powered off. I clutch it in my hand and look up and down the road for approaching traffic. There are no cars in sight.

"Let's go behind the building," I say to Bethy. Her eyes are wide with fright, but she jogs around to the back of the building and tries to look unafraid.

Leaning my back against the wall, I turn the phone on and dial Andrew. He picks up on the second ring.

"Quinn? Everything okay?"

"No." My voice is choked. "I'm in trouble. I need you."

"Where are you?"

I swallow hard. This is harder than I thought it would be. I trusted Bean with Bethy, and that was a mistake. But besides Bethy, Andrew is all I have now, and I know in my heart he'll do everything in his power to help us.

"I'm . . . I don't know for sure. It's called Barra de Potosi. I'm not far from Ixtapa. And things went bad with Bean. I think he'll be coming after us, and Bethy says he has connections to a cartel down here."

Andrew exhales deeply into the phone. "Okay. Are you on the road?"

"I'm in a car with Pennsylvania plates. I'm worried about being easy to find in it."

"Yeah, leave the car."

"We're in a pretty rural place. And we don't blend in. I don't know what to do."

"You need to lay low. And don't turn your phone off because I'm going to use it to pinpoint your location. Try to move and stay as hidden as possible on foot, okay? I'll get someone to you as quickly as possible, and I'm on my way too."

"Andrew?"

"Yeah?"

"If anything happens to me, promise you'll find Bethy and help her."

"Don't even say that. Nothing's going to happen to you, Quinn."

I squeeze my eyes shut and fight back tears. "Just promise me. Please."

After a pause, he says, "I promise."

I breathe easier. "Okay."

"Just stay hidden and don't respond to anyone who doesn't contact you through this phone, okay?"

"Okay."

I hang up, put the phone back in my purse, and sling my

bags over my shoulder.

"We need to walk," I say.

As we move away from the café, the darkness makes it impossible to see more than a couple feet in front of us.

"This is good, right?" Bethy whispers. "It'll be harder for anyone to find us in the dark."

"Yeah," I say softly. "It's good."

We move farther away from the road into rocky terrain. Bethy's thin flip-flops hardly protect her feet, so it's slow going.

I don't want to get my phone out and risk the light being seen, so we just walk in silence for around an hour. My heart is still racing as I replay what went down with Bean. I feel a deep sense of betrayal I can't even process right now.

I feel a squish beneath my shoe and I stop walking, getting a bad feeling when I hear a hissing sound.

"What the fuck is that?" I whisper, bending down.

It's a lizard—and *not* a small one. The hissing and flailing make me wonder if I should let it out from under my shoe. Just as I draw my knife, it manages to wiggle free on its own and it crawls off into the darkness.

If I were alone, I'd sit down and cry for a few minutes. But I have to stay strong for Bethy. We walk aimlessly, and I try not to think about the fact that we have no water and could be walking away from civilization. If Andrew doesn't find us before sunrise, we'll be in a bad spot.

For now, all I can do is put one foot in front of the other. We find smoother ground and my heart rate finally settles. I know we've been walking for at least a few hours when the sound of my phone beeping with a new text makes Bethy jump into the air with alarm.

"It's just my phone, crazypants," I say, scrambling to get it out.

There's a message from an unknown number.

Andrew sent me to help. I'm less than a mile away. Look for the lights and head toward us when you see them.

I breathe a sigh of relief.

"Andrew sent help," I say softly. "Someone's really close. We're supposed to look for their lights."

We stop and look in every direction.

"There," Bethy says, pointing.

There's a tiny speck of light in the distance, and we both walk toward it. Within five minutes, we come across a group of two men and one woman, all dressed in camo and outfitted with bulletproof vests and guns.

"Quinn?" the woman says to me, shining a small flashlight in my direction.

"Yes."

"I'm Vanessa Giano, a friend of Andrew's. We're here to extract you."

"I couldn't be happier to see you," I say with a weak smile.

One of the men gets out a radio and speaks into it. Within a couple minutes, I hear a helicopter approaching. It lands, and we all get on it.

I'm terrified of flying, but I don't feel anything but relief as we're flown away. I wish this was the end of the nightmare, but I know it's not. As much as I want to get Bethy out of here right now, I'm also afraid to return to the States with her.

Chapter Twenty-Four

Andrew

I FEEL LIKE a caged animal in this plane. We've been in the air for hours, and I can't take sitting still for much longer. Vanessa's text an hour ago that she had Quinn and Bethy and was en route to El Paso helped a little, but I need to see Quinn with my own eyes before I'll be able to relax fully.

It's been hell not knowing if she was safe, and getting that frantic phone call from her made the bottom fall out of my world.

"Beginning our descent now, Mr. Wentworth," the pilot says over the private plane's intercom. "Seat belt fastened, please."

"About fucking time," I mutter, sliding the seat belt closed.

It takes forever to land. I'm close to using the seat next to me as a punching bag when finally, we come to a stop.

Quinn texted me that they're in the airport lobby, and I scan faces rapidly as I walk through. Then I see her walking toward me. We break into a run at the same time and meet up in a fierce hug. I lift her feet from the ground and feel her warm breath on my neck.

"You're here," she says, sounding on the verge of tears.

"I'm here. Good luck leaving the country without me ever again."

She laughs softly. When I set her feet back on the ground, she looks over at a wispy brunette girl.

"Bethy, this is Andrew. Andrew, my little sister, Bethy."

She's a pretty, younger version of Quinn with brown hair.

"Hi Bethy," I say, reaching out to shake her hand.

She smiles and shakes my hand back. I realize I should have hugged her. Next time.

"Ladies, we're getting right back on that plane and flying to New York," I say. "They're refueling it now."

"I can't wait to get home," Quinn says.

I love the sound of that. My home is her home now. *Our* home. And it's Bethy's too.

Vanessa is standing to the side, and when I meet her eyes, she walks over to us.

"Everything good now?" she asks.

I reach out and hug her. "I owe you big. Thank you for this."

She laughs and cups my cheek in her palm. "I'm pretty sure I'm still the one who owes you."

I can't tell Quinn because I've sworn to keep the identities of my partners a secret, but Vanessa is one of the five people in the Circle of Six with me. That's the name of the group that funds the second-floor operations at the warehouse.

"See you later, Andrew," Vanessa says.

As soon as she steps back, I sweep Quinn back into my arms and kiss her on the mouth, pouring all the worry and uncertainty of the past few hours into it.

We're both breathless when she breaks the kiss.

"I love you, Quinn," I murmur against her lips.

"I love you, too."

We board the plane then, and Bethy immediately goes to sleep in one of the reclining seats. I cover her with a blanket and sit down next to Quinn. She snuggles against my side and is asleep within a couple minutes.

A FEW HOURS later, I'm carrying Quinn down the hall to our bedroom. Despite sleeping a couple hours on the plane, she's exhausted. I am, too. I put Turner in charge of getting Bethy fed and settled into her room and canceled my day at the office. I'm planning to sleep away the morning with Quinn.

I get her out of her clothes and into one of my T-shirts and lay her on the bed while I strip down to my boxer briefs. When I climb in next to her and pull the covers over us, she opens her eyes and looks at me in the dim light of the room.

"He's my stepfather," she says softly.

"Who is?"

"That's who we're running from. We're from Colorado. My name is Quinn Bradley."

I smile and wrap my palm around her hip. "Your last name's not really Jones?"

She smiles back. "No."

"Why did you leave? What did he do?"

With a soft sigh, she tucks her hair behind her ear. "My mom married him a couple years after my dad died. She'd run through a lot of money, and Paul, my stepdad, is wealthy. I never liked him. I'd just turned sixteen, and we were in the kitchen one day and . . ." She pauses for a couple seconds. "He rubbed his erection against my ass when I was reaching into a kitchen cabinet. Scared the absolute shit out of me. He grabbed me and said I needed to stop shaking my ass in front of him and it was time to do something about it."

A knot of anger forms in my chest. "I'm sorry, Quinn. Did

he . . . ?"

"I grabbed a pan from the stove and hit him over the head with it, and I ran out of the room. He made this crazy roaring sound. I'll never forget it. And then he said, 'You'll pay for that, you little bitch. Run all you want. There's no escaping me.'"

"Jesus, what a prick."

"He is. I found out a few days later what the price was when I caught him in Bethy's room while she was asleep. He'd pulled her covers down, and . . . he was jerking off next to her bed."

"Holy shit."

"I told my mother, and she was so angry at me. She said I was lying and was just mad about her getting remarried. I didn't feel like I had any options. My dad asked me before he died to take care of Bethy always. I couldn't let Paul . . . I felt like we had to run."

"Yeah, I can see why."

Her eyes are drifting closed. "I just wanted you to know. No more secrets."

"No more secrets," I say, kissing her forehead. "Never again."

"There's one more thing I need to tell you," she says softly.

"What is it?"

"My stepfather . . . he's Paul Shriver."

I just look at her for a couple seconds as disbelief sets in. "Paul Shriver? The senator?"

"Yes."

Fuck. This complicates things. I don't want her to know I'm rattled by it, so I kiss her forehead again.

"Just sleep, baby. We're leaving for Europe tomorrow. The three of us. It's over."

Chapter Twenty-Five

Quinn

I STUFF THE last of my toiletries into my suitcase and zip it. It's really happening. I don't have to choose between Andrew and Bethy—now I can have them both.

Dawson took Bethy shopping for clothes and other Paris essentials, so I can pack my things and Andrew's and we can fly out this evening.

I'll miss the warehouse, the shelter, Turner, and Anna. A big part of me will miss this city because, even with its rough edges, it kept Bethy and me together and safe for more than four years.

We weren't safe from hunger, cold, or sickness. We weren't even safe from threats of violence. But those things were better than what Paul had in mind. I think my father would be proud that his sixteen-year-old daughter managed to outsmart a US senator with nothing but brains and $180 of babysitting money in her pocket.

Our stuff is packed, and all I need to do now is pack Midas's few things. We're taking him with us, of course, and I want him to have his bed and favorite blanket.

"Midas, where are you?" I call as I walk into the living room.

I see him curled up on the couch asleep, and I walk up to pet him. Before I reach him, a hand wraps around my waist.

"Hello, Quinn."

It can't be. It can't possibly be. Not here, in my safe place. My home.

I turn and meet the dark, calculating gaze of my stepfather. He takes a piece of paper out of his pocket and unfolds it, grinning. It's a printout of a photo from an online magazine. Andrew is kissing me on the forehead. I'm wearing the cream gown in the photo, so it has to be from the fundraiser we went to. Steve apparently didn't buy all the photos.

I'm not a sixteen-year-old girl anymore. I'll keep my chin high, and I won't let him see me cry.

"Your stalking game is strong," I say, crossing my arms over my chest. "What else do you want me to say?"

"I have to say I'm surprised at you, Quinn. You must have something hot between your thighs to pull Andrew Wentworth."

"Fuck you."

The paper falls from his hand and sails to the ground as he advances toward me, his face twisted into a mask of rage.

"You thought you could outsmart me, you little bitch, but you didn't. I found you. No more running, Quinn."

His hands are outstretched, and I know he's going to choke me. I look around frantically. There's no pan in reach this time. It's just him and me.

I suck in a breath of air and crouch down to lower my center of gravity. He's just a few feet from me when I say the only words that can save me now.

"David Alan Wentworth."

I practically yell it as fear courses through me. I hope it was loud enough. Paul wraps his powerful hands around my neck and squeezes away my ability to breathe.

I try to knee him, but my feet are dangling in the air. I've got no momentum. I'm clawing at his hands around my neck, but it's not enough. His face becomes a swirl of colors that fades to gray. My hands are too weak to fight anymore. I'm fading. My eyes slide closed, and I give in to the pull of darkness.

Chapter Twenty-Six

Quinn

I HEAR A man's voice.

"Quinn? Open your eyes for me. You're safe. Andrew's on his way."

When I lift my eyelids, I see the face of Andrew's security guy Steve. He's kneeling next to me. My hands instinctively go to my throat, which is still burning.

"Don't touch it," Steve says, easing my hands down. "You're okay."

I start to sit up, looking side to side for my stepfather. "Where's Paul?" My words come out in a croak.

"He's restrained. Lie down, okay?"

His tone is so soothing that I let my head fall back down to the couch. My neck is throbbing, and I still feel the terror of not being able to breathe.

Paul is here. He's inside the warehouse. I have to keep my gaze on Steve to calm my pounding heart and remember I'm safe.

A couple minutes later, I hear Andrew yelling my name from the kitchen. It sounds like he just came up from the garage and is looking for me.

"Where is she? Have you got him?" His voice is frantic.

Steve stands up. "She's here. We've got him tied up in your office."

Andrew's gaze lands on me and his eyes widen. "What the fuck happened?"

He bends down and pulls me into his arms. I'm sore, but I need him to hold me tight right now so I don't wince.

"Bethy," I whisper in his ear. "He can't know she's here."

"I texted Dawson on my way here," Andrew whispers back. "He's taking her somewhere safe."

I want to relax, but I can't. The tears come hard and fast. Andrew keeps his arms locked around me as I sob against his pressed white dress shirt.

"It's okay," he says softly. "I'm here now. You're safe."

"You can't protect me from this." It burns my throat to talk.

"Yes, I can. I'll have her out of the country within a few hours. Trust me, okay?"

I nod. "What about Paul?"

"I'll take care of him. You go upstairs and rest."

"I'm coming with you."

Andrew shakes his head. "You don't need to be in there for this, Quinn."

"Yes, I do. We said no secrets, didn't we?"

He draws his brows together in a skeptical look. "Okay, if that's what you want."

"I want to choke the life out of that bastard," I say. "He nearly killed me."

Andrew releases me and looks at Steve. "How the fuck did he get in here?"

"He flashed his Senate ID at Micah and said he had a meeting with you."

"No one gets in here unescorted. *No one.* Fire Micah and

remind him of the NDA he signed when you hired him."

"Yes, sir," Steve says. "But . . . I think you should fire me as well."

"I just might," Andrew snaps. "This shouldn't have gotten by you."

Steve nods and gives me a pained look. "It's my fault."

"What do you mean?" I ask.

"We found a printout of a photo from an online magazine on the living room floor. It's from that event you were photographed at. I was supposed to buy them all, and obviously, I missed one. That must be how he found you. I'm sorry."

Andrew sighs heavily. "Let's just clean this fucking mess up, okay?"

He takes my hand, and the three of us walk back to Andrew's office. The closer we get, the stronger my sense of foreboding becomes. Looks like Paul was right. There *was* no escaping him.

At least Bethy's safe. I clutch Andrew's hand and remind myself that if Paul can't find her, I can't get into legal trouble. Hopefully. Paul is a very powerful man.

Paul is scowling at us from the floor, his hands and feet bound with thin ropes.

"I demand to be released," he says. "You are holding a United States senator captive."

Andrew looks unconcerned. "I'm holding an intruder in my home until the authorities arrive."

"You didn't call the police," Paul says, practically snarling. "But I did before I got here. I said if they didn't hear back from me within an hour, they should come here to investigate."

"Nice of you to report your invasion of my home," Andrew says. "Saves me the trouble."

"I was let inside."

"Under what pretense?"

I cut in. "What do you want, Paul? I'm an adult now, and I want nothing to do with you or my mother."

"We wrote you off a long time ago," he says with a sneer. "It's Bethy we want back. God knows what you've put her through."

"I saved her from sexual assault by you, you sick bastard," I fire back.

"Let me go," Paul says to Andrew. "You don't know who Quinn really is. She's a very troubled young woman."

Andrew reaches down to the ropes tied around Paul's wrists behind his back and hauls him up to his feet. He slams him face first into the wall, and Paul cries out in pain.

"Keep your fucking mouth shut," Andrew says in a low, menacing tone.

Steve looks at the screen of his phone and glances up at Andrew. "There are people out front. Should we let them in?"

"Might be the police," Andrew says, looking at me. "Sure, let them in."

We all file out of Andrew's office and into the living room. Paul actually hops since his ankles are bound. I keep my hand locked with Andrew's, needing to feel his presence next to me.

When we get to the living room, the front door opens and Dawson steps inside with Bethy. His eyes slide to Paul's for just a second. It's almost imperceptible.

"What the fuck are you doing here?" Andrew demands, glaring at Dawson.

I look at my sister and feel light-headed. She's seen Paul, and the color has drained from her face.

"I'm just bringing Bethy back," Dawson says. "Is there a problem?"

"I texted you other instructions," Andrew says sharply.

"I must have missed that."

Andrew shakes his head. "What the hell have you done,

Dawson? You sold us out to this guy?"

Dawson scoffs. "It was only a matter of time, anyway. Quinn's been angling to take over for me since she moved in here." He turns to me. "I wish I would've kept walking when I saw you having a breakdown on that sidewalk."

"Get Quinn and Bethy out of here," Andrew says to Steve.

Steve nods and Andrew turns to me.

"He'll keep you safe," he says in a low tone.

"You aren't taking my daughter," Paul says to Steve, wrestling with the bonds on his wrists. "You don't want to kidnap a senator's daughter, do you?"

Steve ignores him. I go to Bethy and wrap my arms around her. She's shaking. This was supposed to be over, and now it's blowing up in our faces.

"We'll be okay," I say, trying to convince both her and myself.

But then I hear voices at the front door, and I realize it won't. It's the police. Paul apparently wasn't bluffing about calling them.

Bethy bursts into tears. I'm too upset to cry at this point. I'm just numb. We were so close to freedom, but now it's all over.

Chapter Twenty-Seven

Andrew

PAUL SHRIVER IS a Grade A asshole. I knew it already from what Quinn told me and from what the private investigator I put on him came up with. But he proves it again when the police walk into the warehouse.

"I'm Senator Paul Shriver," he says arrogantly. "And that's my daughter, Bethy Bradley. She was kidnapped from my home four years ago."

"I am *not* your daughter," Bethy says.

Quinn has her arms wrapped protectively around her sister, and my love for her grows stronger. She's the most selfless person I've ever known.

"She's been brainwashed," Paul says, shaking his head with disgust.

I speak to the three uniformed NYPD officers in my living room. "This man broke in to my home and choked my girlfriend. I have video."

Paul's eyes widen. I hope he's shitting his pants right now. I decide to sweeten this moment a little more and show Quinn this bastard's not untouchable.

"I know more about you than you realize, Senator," I tell him. "Your dealings with Cargill. Melissa Shaw. Want me to enlighten everyone?"

"No." He gives me a murderous glare.

"Bethy's staying with us." I leave no room for doubt. "I'm certain the missing person claim will be dropped. And since that's settled, I don't think we have any need for the police, do we, Paul?"

After a few seconds of silence, he says, "I suppose not. Untie me, and I'll leave with the officers."

"Whoa," one of the officers says, putting up a hand. "We aren't leaving here without getting some questions answered."

"It was all a misunderstanding," Paul says. "I'm the one who called you, and I apologize, officers."

"We need to talk to the girl alone," the officer says.

Quinn gives me a questioning look, and I nod. The officers take Bethy into the kitchen and talk to her privately.

Leaning close to whisper in my ear, Quinn asks, "Who's Melissa Shaw?"

"I'll tell you later."

She nods and wraps her arms protectively around herself. I pull her into my arms and hold her close until the officers return to the living room with Bethy a couple minutes later.

"Okay," one of them says, shaking his head. "If no one wants to file a complaint, I guess we're done here."

"Take this piece of shit with you," I say, nodding toward Paul.

"Bethy, your mother misses you," Paul says. "At least call her and let her know you're safe."

Bethy shakes her head. "You can tell her I'm safe. I don't want to talk to her."

Steve cuts the ties from Paul's hands, and he leaves with the cops. Quinn gives me a questioning look as soon as the door closes behind them.

"That's it?" she asks, her brow furrowed with disbelief.

"That's it. I put a PI team on him last night, right after you told me his name. He's done both unethical and illegal things to benefit an oil company that cuts him six-figure checks every quarter. He also beat a prostitute last year and paid her to keep quiet about it."

Quinn shakes her head sadly. "I can't say I'm surprised."

"Does this mean we're not going to Paris?" Bethy asks, looking back and forth between Quinn and me.

"We can still go if you want," I say. "Might be nice to get away for a while."

"Can we wait? I need to catch my breath," Quinn says. "Between Paul and Dawson and just . . . everything, I'm exhausted."

I nod, thinking about what needs to be done now that Dawson and Micah have been fired. I need to call my attorney and reprogram the facial recognition program to alert security at a high level if either one of them comes onto the property.

"Bethy can go to school now," Quinn says, tears shining in her eyes. "And we can get IDs in our real names. I never thought—"

She presses a palm to her mouth, and tears spill onto her cheeks. It's all hitting her now.

"I never really thought it would be over," she says softly. "Not unless they found us and we had to go back."

I take her in my arms and hold her close to me. "It's all over now. You guys won't have to look over your shoulders ever again."

She cries harder, and I realize how rarely I've seen this vulnerable side of her. I'm ready to show her my vulnerabilities, too. When Bethy goes upstairs to rest in her room and Steve returns from securing the warehouse, I sit down on the couch and pull Quinn onto my lap.

"You know why I live here?" I ask.

"You mean in New York?"

I shake my head. "No, the warehouse."

"Because you like security."

"That's true," I admit. "And I also needed space for . . . the upstairs stuff. But I need to live and work at the ground level. I have a thing about tall buildings because of 9/11."

She presses her lips to my neck in a soft kiss. "That's completely understandable."

"Same with windows. I've always been a little obsessed with security because . . . I don't even know why. My dad's gone, and it made me feel closer to him to protect myself from having the same thing happen to me."

"I don't think anyone would ever blame you for that."

I sigh against her soft hair. "I just wanted to tell you I've got my weaknesses, you know?"

"Thank you. I owe you my life, Andrew. And Bethy's, too. No one's ever had my back the way you do."

"I always will. You're stuck with me."

She laughs, and I feel her warm breath against my neck. "You're stuck with me, too. I love you."

"I love you, too. You make me want to be a better person."

"You're already one of the best."

I close my eyes and take in her soft, sweet scent and the warmth of her against me. I never thought the ice that formed in my heart on 9/11 could be melted, but Quinn has changed everything.

After my father died, I started fighting because of the hate inside me. But I realize now that love is the only thing that's really worth fighting for. Quinn broke down my walls, and I never want to put them back up.

Chapter Twenty-Eight

Quinn

IT'S SATURDAY, AND Andrew's not working. I hope this is the start of many two-day weekends for us. This morning, I woke to the brush of his short beard on my thighs beneath the sheets in our bed. After giving me two toe-curling orgasms from slow, sensual sex, he told me to get a quick shower because he had plans for the day.

We took Bethy to a local diner for breakfast and then shopped for furnishings for her bedroom and clothes for when she starts school next week. I was surprised Andrew endured three hours at Old Navy, but he was a champ. He wants Bethy to know he cares, and that means the world to me.

It's been easy to adjust to this new life. I'm relaxed all the time now and happier than I've ever thought possible. When we get back home, Bethy and I take Midas for a walk and I feel light.

"I'm going to be the dumbest sophomore ever," Bethy says softly. Midas is sniffing a bench on the sidewalk, and I stop walking and turn to my sister.

"You will not," I say firmly. "The tutors Andrew hired will catch you up in no time."

She gives me a nervous smile. "I'm mostly excited. I can't believe this is our life now."

We resume walking, and I put an arm around her shoulders. "I know. It's pretty incredible. But I'm going back to school, too. I'm going to get a GED and then start college. I want to prove to myself I can do it and someday do some kind of work that matters. Don't ever plan on finding a man to take care of you. In a good relationship, you take care of each other."

Bethy looks over at me, wearing a somber expression. "I've never thanked you for what you did. You gave up everything . . ." Her eyes fill with tears. "Just to protect me."

"*Just*?" I tighten my hold on her shoulders. "Protecting you was worth it. And we're both stronger because of what we've been through. More compassionate, too. Never look down on others because you have more. It's just opportunities and circumstances that divide the haves from the have-nots most of the time."

"I want to be a doctor," Bethy says softly. "Maybe work at a clinic for the homeless."

"You'd be amazing at that," I say as we climb the steps to the warehouse. I key in the code and we walk inside, where the savory scents of beef and spices greet us.

"Hey," Andrew says, looking up from the kitchen island where he's chopping something on a cutting board. "I'm making beef stew."

"Yum." I shed my coat, walk into the kitchen, and wrap my arms around his waist from behind. "Mmm, you're warm."

He turns and kisses my forehead. "We've got company for dinner."

"Hi, Quinn," Andrew's mother says from the other side of the kitchen.

"Oh." I unwrap myself from around Andrew and look at her warily. "Hi."

She's peeling apples in front of a kitchen counter, and she puts down the knife and turns to me with a slight smile. After our last encounter, I have a sense of dread in the pit of my stomach.

"I want to apologize to you," she says, her eyes on mine. "I was rude and judgmental. When Andrew told me how you came to be in New York and what you've been through, I was ashamed of myself. I admire your strength and courage, Quinn, and I'd love a second chance."

I'm taken aback. For a few seconds, I just look at her. Then I glance at Andrew and see hope in his bright blue eyes.

"Of course," I finally manage, clearing my throat. "I'd like that."

She nods and then introduces herself to Bethy. I'm floored when she wraps her arms around my sister in a hug.

I stand next to Andrew at the island, picking up the pile of carrot peelings and putting them in a bowl to throw away. He turns to me, and when I look up at him, he leans my way and kisses me softly on the lips.

"Thank you," he whispers.

I stand on my tiptoes and lean up to kiss him again. "Love you."

"Love you, too."

I see emotions swimming in his eyes. There's affection, lust, and tenderness. I can tell just from his gaze that we'll be going to sleep sweaty after incredible sex tonight.

I've gone from my lowest point to my highest in a matter of months. From feeling forlorn about the future to feeling hopeful about it. My Prince Charming isn't always sweet, and he's still learning how to love. But he's mine, I'm his, and I wouldn't change a thing.

Epilogue

One year later

Quinn

ANDREW GIVES ME a tight smile as the elevator begins its ascent. He's squeezing my hand and tapping his polished black dress shoe on the elevator floor.

"We don't have to do this," I remind him.

"I'm good." He doesn't look at me when he says it, so I know he's wound tight. And he's *not* good.

His idea to go to the top of the Empire State Building surprised me. A couple weeks ago, he told me to put this on my schedule for tonight, and my heart had squeezed from the earnest look on his face.

"The . . . Empire State Building?" I'd said, my brows arched. "Really?"

"Yes."

It wasn't that Andrew never went onto the upper floors of tall buildings. He often had to for work meetings or to visit his mom's place. But this was different. He'd chosen this place to face his fears. Being at the top of a building more than one thousand feet tall—and on the outside, no less—wasn't something he'd done since before his father died.

"Did I tell you I finished writing that paper?" I ask him, hoping to distract him.

He looks down at me. "Yeah? I'd like to read it."

"Of course. Your friend was a great resource for it."

I'd interviewed one of Andrew's former business partners from the Circle of Six. He was a counterterrorism expert who helped me understand the current political climate in the Middle East. And when he'd told me about losing his son on 9/11, I'd seen the same pain in his eyes I saw in Andrew's when he spoke of his dad.

When Andrew withdrew from the Circle of Six eight months ago, he'd turned a corner in his grieving process. Killing terrorists had never brought him the peace he sought. Now he honored his father's memory in a new way.

The David Wentworth Foundation funded a summer camp for children who'd lost a parent. We were overseeing construction of new cabins on a large piece of property upstate we'd bought for the camp. The massive main lodge would be done in time for the first group of campers this summer, and it included a suite for us.

The elevator slows and then stops. Our elevator attendant nods and we step out, Andrew keeping his hold on my hand. He called in a favor to get us an after-hours private trip up here, so we're all alone.

It's a brisk winter evening, and my breath clouds in front of my face as I take in the view and sigh.

"It's spectacular," I say.

Andrew looks out over his city silently. His eyes pool with emotion, and I bring his large hand up to my lips to kiss his knuckles.

"Thinking about my dad," he says softly.

"He'd be proud of you right now."

A small smile plays on his lips as he looks down at me. "He would've loved you." His smile broadens. "You know what feels good?"

"What?"

"I'm not thinking about his death. I'm thinking about a story he told me one night when I couldn't sleep." His eyes dance with happiness. "I was six or seven at the time, I think."

"What was it about?"

He looks from side to side, taking in the view of the skyline again. "It was about this place." He turns back to me and brushes a thumb over my lips. "This is where he proposed to my mom."

When he reaches into his pocket, my heart pounds wildly. As he gets down on one knee, I blink and feel hot tears on my cold cheeks.

"Andrew," I whisper.

Tears shine in his eyes. "Quinn Bradley, I love you with all my heart. You made this controlling bastard into a lovesick puppy, and I couldn't be happier about it. Will you marry me?"

I swipe a thumb across my cheeks and nod wildly. "Yes, Andrew, a thousand times *yes*."

He stands and pulls me into his arms, swinging me around. I feel like my heart may burst from the joy of this moment.

When he sets me back on the ground, he slides a simple square solitaire in a platinum band onto my finger.

"My mother's," he says, his voice hoarse with emotion.

Gina Wentworth has become a mother to me in every way. Like Andrew, she's pure gold beneath her hard façade.

"I'm honored to wear it," I say, wiping away another round of tears. "It's perfect."

The elevator attendant is approaching with a glass of champagne in each hand. He passes them to us and then walks back over to the elevator to allow us privacy.

"You thought I was nervous about being up here," Andrew says to me, "but I was more nervous about proposing."

I lean in close, looking up at his dark-stubbled face. "How could you not know I would say yes?"

"You never know 'til the deal's done," he says with a boyish shrug. "And I wanted it to be perfect."

"It was."

"To us," he says, clinking his glass lightly against mine.

"To us." I sip the cold, bubbly champagne and admire the sparkling ring on my finger.

"You know, I thought I was saving you from a life on the streets," Andrew says, smiling wryly and shaking his head, "but it was you who saved me."

I shrug and smile at him. "I'm a modern-day Cinderella. I think we should take turns saving each other."

Andrew kisses me gently. "We do."

"And we will."

"Forever."

"You don't mind if I wear my hunting knife underneath my wedding dress, do you?" I ask with a playful smile.

He cocks an amused brow. "We may need to discuss that."

Author's Note

THANK YOU FOR reading His! If you enjoyed it, I would really appreciate a review at the site you purchased it from. It doesn't need to be long or detailed—anything helps.

If you're on Facebook, I'd love to have you in my group Rothert's Readers, where I share the latest on my work and do special giveaways.

About the Author

BRENDA ROTHERT LIVES in Central Illinois with her husband and three sons. She was a daily print journalist for nine years, during which time she enjoyed writing a wide range of stories.

These days Brenda writes Contemporary Romance. She loves to hear from readers.

Connect with Brenda

www.brendarothert.com

Facebook

Twitter

Goodreads

Pinterest

Books by Brenda Rothert

NOW SERIES
Now and Then
Now and Again
Now and Forever

FIRE ON ICE SERIES
Bound
Captive
Edge
Release
Drive

ON THE LINE SERIES
Killian
Bennett
Liam (coming soon)

LOCKHART BROTHERS SERIES
Deep Down
In Deep
Drawn Deeper (coming soon)

STANDALONES
Unspoken
Barely Breathing
Blown Away
Dirty Work (with Chelle Bliss) (coming soon)

Acknowledgements

I'M GRATEFUL TO everyone who helped make this book what it is. It took me some time to wrap my arms around this story and its characters, and as always, I had lots of help.

Beta readers Janett Gomez, Michelle Tan, Chantal Gemperle and Chelle Northcutt gave me feedback and encouragement that kept me moving toward the finish line. I'm so lucky to have these ladies on my team.

Editor Lisa Hollett gave this story its polish. Her attention to detail is fantastic and I couldn't ask for a better line editor.

Rosa Sharon gave this book a good proofreading, as did Joanne Thompson. (Thanks, ladies!)

Jessica Estep of Inkslinger PR helped spread the word about this book and also helped me keep things on track for a smooth release. My assistant Pam Million helped with ARCs, organization and just being an awesome friend.

Sara Eirew took my gorgeous cover photo and designed my stunning cover. I love, love, love working with Sara. It's stress-free and I always know I'll get a cover I adore.

Christine Borgford of Perfectly Publishable did my interior design and formatting. She is the best formatter in the world, hands-down. Possibly the universe.

Pam Carrion keeps the energy high in my reader group,

Rothert's Readers. I just love pretty much everything about her.

To everyone in Rothert's Readers and every blogger who promos and supports my work—I could not do this without you. It means everything.

And thanks to you, dear reader, for buying this book and supporting me so I can keep writing more. This career is a dream.

Huge hugs and thanks to my husband and three boys, who put up with my night writing, laundry slacking, cereal for dinner ways.

www.ingramcontent.com/pod-product-compliance
Lightning Source LLC
Chambersburg PA
CBHW060150180626
46813CB00007B/2691
* 9 7 8 0 9 9 6 8 4 9 8 5 2 *